# A Walk With A Lion

I0653340

Sanket Patel

First published in 2017 by

Becomeshakespeare.com
Wordit Content Design & Editing Services Pvt Ltd
Unit - 26, Building A-1, Nr Wadala RTO, Wadala (East),
Mumbai 400037, India
T:+91 8080226699
This book has been fully funded by the Wordit Art Fund.

Wordit Art Fund helps deserving authors publish their work by providing monetary support. To apply for funding, please visit us at
www.BecomeShakespeare.com

ISBN: 978-93-86487-17-9

For all those,

who is a soldier,
who fights when told
and wins when fights.

dedicated to real heroes
Indian Army

A Walk With A Lion

# CONTENTS

# PROLOGUE
## [VIMAL]

Dead.

That's what Shiv is now, dead.

It only took a moment for the doctor to say that my best friend is dead, but he has no idea of how long it is going to be for me before I truly believe he is gone.

How can I?

He is my best friend.

He is my brother.

He is my half-life.

And today he is gone.

Sometimes, we never know the value of a moment until it becomes a memory, and today, when he is finally gone, his memories flashes in front of my eyes. We never thought that we were making memories, we thought that we were having fun, and passing the time, but today, when he is finally gone, I realize how important those memories are. It was not only my friend who had died; it was something of me that had died along with him.

I looked at everyone who shed tears. Aastha, Smit, Visha, Brijesh, Jigar, Minal, Rajan, Bhargav, Brinda, Bhoomi, Rohan, Dimpal, Nehal, Shivani, all fourteen of them were mourning for his death. But I wasn't. I was not going to cry nor was I going to shed a tear. If I cry and let my tears loose, it will mean that I am finally letting him go, and that, I am not going to do. He is not going anywhere. He is staying in my heart for now and forever. It doesn't matter what others say and what others do, I am not letting him go.

"It's okay to cry, Vimal," Minal said to me, "It doesn't make you weak."

"No," I replied. "I won't cry."

I looked at her as a tear ran down her cheek. She was trying to control herself but her every effort was in vain. One after other, tears started making their way out through her eyes. Soon, she was sobbing and I tried to calm her down.

"You too, shouldn't cry." I said to Minal. "That's what he would have wanted."

She nodded and tried to control her tears. After few moments, she was calm again and I left her in silence. I stood up from my seat and walked to Shivani, who was in love with my best friend. As soon as I had taken my seat next to her,she started sobbing, and I had to wrap my arms around her to calm her down.

"How could this happen to him?" She said, "He was so nice and so good to everyone, why would someone do something like this to him?"

"I don't know," I replied. "Maybe, the people we care about most in life are taken from us too soon."

In seconds, her sobbings and tears were too much for me to control and I had to call Visha and Aastha to calm her down. Both of them took her in their arms and all three of them cried together.

"Was this grief that we were all feeling?" I thought to myself. "Is this just a natural response to losing someone or something that's important to you? No. This isn't. This is far from grief. This is love. This is all really just love. All that love that we want to give but cannot. All of that unspent love gathered up in the corner of our eyes, the lump in our throat, that hollow part in our chest, this all is just love with no place to go."

"Vimal," Smit spoke, "We need to call uncle."

I nodded to him. He was right; we have to inform uncle and aunt about this. They were his family, his only family, and they need to know about this.

I walked away from them to have some silence while I call. In the corridor, I dialed uncle's cell number. He was busy on another call. After few minutes, I called him again. Again, he was busy and I ended the call. I left him a message to call me as soon as possible. After that, I returned to my friends who were all mourning on their friend's death.

Many people enters and leaves our life and we forget everything about them, but wecannot do anything to get rid of the best people in our life. They leave the ass prints on the sofa of our souls. For friends, goodbyes are not forever, goodbyes are not the end; it simply means that, they'll miss the other until they meet again. But this goodbye, that he had given me, was going to last beyond forever, beyond the end of my life.

He and I, we used to be together, always together every day, and losing him now feels like losing a part of myself. I cannot believe this is the end of our journey together. We were supposed to be together forever and he had betrayed me by leaving me all alone in this world. Despite me being pain in the ass, he still liked to be with me, I was stupid and crazy and still he liked to be with me. We never did stupid things, alone, we laughed at each other when we fell down, I wouldn't have dared to be this weird without him, and today, at the saddest moment of my life, when the person who gave me my best memories, became a memory, I realized that losing a friend is most painful thing in the world, even more painful than losing a true love.

"Vimal, what happened?" Nehal asked. "Did you talk with uncle?"

"No." I replied. "He was busy but I have left him a message to call me as soon as possible."

She nodded and remained standing next to me. I looked around at the friends who were still crying and mourning and was in shock with the news of their best friend's death. Their pain, their grief, their loss, everything, I could feel it. The mere mention of his name brings the emptiness and loneliness in my heart. However, I have made my peace with it now. I had almost lost him before, but that time, I had saved him from the death. Twice actually, twice before had I almost lost him, but he came back and stayed with me. We bonded and made promises to be together. A day barely passed without us seeing each other and we kept our promises, but now, he had broken his promise and left me all alone in this world. His absence has gone through me like a thread through a needle. Everything I have drawn in my memories is stitched with his colors. But now, these colors are empty without him and the thread is all alone without the needle.

Moments were passing by and the shock of our best friend's death was fading away. We were finally accepting the fact that our friend is dead and is never coming back. We have to be strong now when

Shiv's uncle and aunt comes to the hospital. If we had lost a friend, they had lost a son. And the loss that they will feel, will be of far more strength than that of ours.

We stood there, in silence, when a nurse came to us and spoke.

"Who is Vimal?" She asked.

"I am Vimal." I said.

"Doctor wants to see you." She said.

"I'll be right there." I replied and she left me.

"I'll be back in a moment." I said to others and left there company.

"What could it be?" I thought. "Maybe, now I'll know the reason behind my best friend's death. No one had told anything to us about his disappearance. For past two days, he was missing and on third day, when he finally shows up, he shows up with wounds and bullets in his body. Doctor takes him to surgery, removes all the bullets from his body, and takes care of all of his wounds. Then they say that he will be all right in few hours, but after an hour or so, they give this dreadful news of his death to us. What was this all that was going on with him? Whatever it was, I am going to get some answers now."

I walked through the corridor and opened the door of the doctor's office. There was no one in the office except for a nurse who was going through the cupboard full of medicines.

"Where's the doctor?" I asked her.

"He's gone to the patient's room." She replied.

"Which patient?" I asked.

"The one from the forest." She said.

"Ok." I said and left the doctor's room.

Again, I walked through the corridor and made my way towards Shiv's room. I told myself that I am not going to cry when I see Shiv's body. I can hold on to myself and be strong. That is what he would have wanted me to do, be strong.

Step after step, I got close to his room. With every step, I felt heavy at my heart and felt like giving away to tears. Finally, I was in front of Shiv's room and I told myself to be strong. I cleared my thoughts and held my composure before opening the door.

Then, I opened the door.

I had thought that I would break down and give away to tears on seeing the dead body of my best friend. However, instead of tears and breakdown, I stood there in shock. Hatred and anger was all that had filled my mind. There was no tears, no heartache, no breakdowns, but pure hatred and anger.

I had no idea of what had happened to Shiv and how this had happened to him, but whatever had lead him to this; someone was surely going to pay. With that very thought in my mind, I entered the room to pay someone for all that had happened, and closed the door behind me.

"There is nothing that could be done now," I said, "nothing, but pay."

# CHAPTER 1
## April 2006, [SHIV]

I walked down the stairs of Santram Mandir, and started walking towards the parking stand. I made my way through the crowd, colliding with all the devotees who had come to visit the temple. In the distance, I saw many more joining in the crowd and I was not even slightly amazed of them.

Santram Mandir, being famous in all over the state, was home to Santram Maharaj and was located in the town of Nadiad. The temple, which once was at the outskirts, was now the heart of the town. Many devotees from all over the state visit the temple throughout the year.

Once I had reached the parking stand, I took out the keys from my pocket to unlock the cycle. After unlocking the cycle, I started my way out. On the way, I met many other students from my school. They were all here praying for the exams. Although my exams were also going on, my reason behind the visit to the temple was different. I had more important and serious matters in my hand than exams, which along with efforts from my side, requires as much blessings as possible for the accomplishment.

After I had made it through the gates of the temple, I climbed on the cycle and started paddling for my next destination. In few minutes, I reached a 75 feet tall building of Lord Shiva in sitting posture. I stood there and watched the premises of Shri Kalyandham with amazement. Every time I see it, Ithink of it coming to life and walking away.

After few moments of staring the structure, I walked into a forty-one meters high temple of Shri Keshav Bhavani. Inside, it had fifty-one different idols and eighteen different coats. The inner walls of the temple had the stanzas of Shri Chand Path engraved on marble. There are hundred and eight spire pots in the temple and Maha Shree Yantra made of silver and gold, which is more than 1.2 meters tall and weighs two hundred and seventy five kg. Once I had bowed my head in front of every single idol, I started walking towards Shri Kalyandham. After completing my prayers in Shri Kalyandham, I left the temple premises, unlocked my bicycle, and rode towards my school, which was few minutes from the temple.

The school premises was near railway station. There was a single narrow road for entering and leaving the school. Therefore, students faced consistent problem of traffic on the road whenever school hours started and ended. I parked my bicycle two blocks from the school so that I do not have to face traffic when I leave. After I had locked my bicycle, I walked past the blocks to the school entrance. There I met Vimal who was eagerly waiting for me. The grin on his face told me I was about to face some teasing.

"So how's the preparation going, huh?" he said with a smirk.

"Fine, I guess! Let's go!" I replied joining in the smile.

The school had three inter-connected buildings with two of them having three levels and one of them having five levels. These buildings interconnected in such a way that it formed a C letter, and were the highest-level buildings I had ever seen in my life until then. All this school buildings were currently over-crowded with students.

School grounds too, were swarming with students. Some of them were running, some were studying, whereas some of them were playing cricket with exam pad and ball made from their handkerchiefs. We made our way through all of them for my examination hall.

By the time we had reached the examination hall, few students had already occupied their seats. I directly walked to my desk waving my hand on the way to few of them whom I knew. I settled down on my desk and Vimal on his, which were few benches from mine. Then, he settled his eyes on me and I settled my eyes on the gate.

Minutes ticked by and my anxiousness grew with every passing second. I was waiting for Vaishavi and she had still not arrived. I started wondering if she would have tied her hair in a ponytail as usual or would have tied it in a bun as she occasionally did. I thought of her, how she looked in a ponytail and compared her looks in ponytail and in bun. In both cases, she appeared beautiful to me. Still I wondered, in which look she would be today.

Anxiousness was taking over me and waiting for her was like eternity to me. However, that eternity soon came to end with her arrival. Dressed in the regular school uniform and ponytail, Vaishavi appeared as if she had walked down the earth directly from heaven. Only thing that she needed is those white feathery wings to complete herself as an angel from the heaven. She was the most beautiful girl I can dream of, and god could ever make.

On realizing that I was staring at her, I glanced away in the direction where Vimal sat. He was smirking out of control. I do not know why but I smiled. It appeared as if new bolts of energy had just entered into me. Joy overflowed my heart and on having no control over it, I kept my head on desk so that no one else can see my face blushing.

I don't even remember when it all had started. Vaishavi and I were in same class since primaries. I don't know when I got attracted to her. Every single day she appeared more beautiful to me than the previous day. In addition, her beauty pulled me towards her. Every day it got difficult for me to control my emotions. It was very hard for me to not let my emotions overtake my mind. Still, I kept it within me. However now, it is high time for me. I cannot control my feelings and the only way to solve this is by telling her how I felt for her.

Today's exam is the last exam for me in this school. In fact, it will be the last time that I'll be coming to the school. From next year onwards, I will be moving down to a boarding school in Ahmedabad, which means that, I will not see Vaishavi anymore.

'Today's the last day in the school, if you don't tell her now; you will never get a second chance for it. This is now or never chance for you.' – This is what Vimal had told me.

I had refused to the idea, but then he told me that if I do not do it, he would. Having no other option in my hand, I had agreed to his idea and come up with a plan to tell her about my feelings.

I have prepared myself for it. I have rehearsed my proposal for at least thousand times in front of him. He had suggested some shyaris and romantic lines that I thought was a bullshit. I wanted it to be simple and not too filmy.

In the morning, I had prayed at every single temple in the town and there was no reason for failure of our plan. I will know the result soon, I thought. The only thing now I need to do is wait until examination gets over.

When I lifted up my head again, everyone had arrived. I saw Vaishavi seating on her place that was in column next to mine, and five rows before me. She was on second bench and in front of the gate. I acted as if I was gazing out. However, most of time, I caught myself staring at her.

Finally, to control my eyes, I turned my eyes from her, lowered my head to the desk, and closed down my eyes. Later when I opened my eyes, examiner had already arrived and was distributing the exam sheets to students. Once examiner had distributed exam sheets, he walked to the door and stood there. After few minutes, a bell rang which signaled that exams had commenced and duration of exams ends in two and a half hours.

Everyone started writing the papers and so did I. However, unlike others, I was concentrating on Vaishavi instead of exams. I occasionally stole a glance at her to check whether she was still writing or had left the room. Minutes passed by and soon, students started leaving the examination hall. Few more minutes passed and Vaishavi left the examination hall. I thought of leaving the hall. I turned around and looked at Vimal. He signaled a nod at me. I sat for few more minutes and then I gave my exam sheets to examiner, and left the hall. Minutes later, Vimal came out. We knew where she would be at that moment. Therefore, we started our way to the cycle stand.

We reached the cycle stand and as Vimal had predicted, she was there with her friends gossiping and laughing. We made our way through cycles until the point where we could hear them clearly. We stood there in between cycles and knelt down in front of one. In few minutes, all of them departed and were on their way to their home.

"Get ready, go!" Vimal said.

I ran to my cycle, climbed over it, and followed after her. Vimal joined me on his cycle and we started following her. I was still hesitating in reaching out to her. I was still afraid of what might come next. Still, we kept on following her keeping safe distance between us.

As I followed her, I saw that her water bottle, which she kept in the side pocket, came loose and fell on the ground. She was not aware of that. Vimal picked up the bottle and gave it to me.

"Go and give it to her." Vimal ordered.

"And then?" I asked.

"And then what?" He asked.

"What am I supposed to do after that?"

"Oh man, just tell her how you feel about her. That is all. If she says yes, signal me, I'll get you the card and the rose."

"You got card and rose?"

"Yes. Someone had to act like grown up."

"Wait, if you have the card and the rose, give it now. What am I supposed to do with it after the proposal?"

"No man, she gets those only if she says yes. If she says no, we could use them on the other girl."

I gave him an evil eye while he grinned.

"Go now!" he said.

I paddled my cycle and called out for her. On hearing her name, she stopped and turned around to see who was calling out for her.

Somehow, I thought, god had arranged this all thing, so that I could tell her what I was planning to do for the whole day.

I stopped my cycle next to her and gave the water bottle to her.

"You dropped this back there on the road!" I said.

"Oh! Thanks!" she said taking the water bottle from my hand.

I stood there in silence not knowing what to do next. I was feeling nervous and was not sure of how to initiate the topic. My heart was already beating faster and my mind was thinking of ways of initiating the talk. I looked at Vimal who was standing at a pan-wala's, waiting for my signal. I wished he had been with me backing me up at the task in hand.

"So! I will leave now. Thanks once again." She said.

Saying that, Vaishavi kept her water bottle in the side pocket where it belonged and was about to leave when I stopped her.

"Vaishavi wait!" I said. "I have something that I want to talk with you."

"Hmm....what's it...?" she asked.

"Ummm...It's something...ummm..." I started talking, still not sure of how to express all that things that I felt for her.

"What's it Shiv? Speak it up! Don't hesitate!" She said.

I gathered my strength to tell her how I felt for her. However, all that I got in return was nervousness. The more I thought about it, the more I got nervous. Although there was no turning back now, I still wished I had not thought of this all propose thing.

"Shiv...What is it? Tell me! Do not think about it. Just tell me what you want to!"

"Ummm...I don't know where to start..." I started. "...It's something about me and...ummm...you...ummm..."

"Shiv, I'm going! Whatever it is that you want to tell, tell me when you are ready. Bye!"

"Wait Vaishavi…" I said, as she started moving. "I'll tell you."

She stopped and folded her hands and stared directly into my eyes.

"Yes now! Speak out whatever it is." She said.

I closed my eyes so that I do not have to face her.

"Vaishavi, what I want to tell you will sound a bit weird or strange or embarrassing or anything that is not pleasant, but still, I have to tell you this because this might be the last time we see each other. You know we are in same class from beginning and have almost grown together until now. Unfortunately, now our paths will be separate. From next year onwards, I will be attending a boarding school in Ahmedabad. And before I leave and move on to next school, I want to tell you that I…"

I paused and again thought of the words that I was about to speak. I opened my eyes and looked at her .

"Vaishavi, I want to tell you that I'm madly in love with you."

My words echoed in my ears long after I had said them. It appeared as if time had slowed down. I was waiting for her to respond but she remained silent. I tried to look at her but could not make an eye contact with her. She was too trying to avoid the eye contact.

"Vaishavi, I know this is not an age for falling in love and feelings and all that, but believe me, I couldn't stop it. The more I try to hide my feelings for you, the more I fall for you, and, to stop that, I had no other option but to tell you how I feel about you. I know that I might not be the best person around but I will love you with all my heart in a way that no one else could. I just want you to keep trust in me and say yes, say yes to me."

I was waiting for her to respond but all she did is remain silent.

"Say something Vaishavi!" I said.

Instead, she remained silent.

We both stood there in silence. I had nothing to say anymore and she might be confused or something for not speaking a single word. This might be too much for her to take in, or maybe, she might be thinking of a way to say that she too loves me. I had no idea what was going on in her head, but whatever it was, it was freaking the hell out of me.

"Vaishavi, take your time." I said. "You can tell me your answer later. I will wait. Right now, you should go back to your home. Your parents might be waiting for you. In addition, I too need to get back to my home. I will see you later. Bye."

I stood there for a moment. When she remained silent, I started my way back towards my house, wondering what she might be thinking right now.

"Shiv…" she called out.

I stopped and turned back to her.

"Yes…?" I asked.

"Shiv…" she said. "I am sorry! It will not be possible for me to have anything like that with you. I have reasons of my own. It would be better if you forget me and move on. Bye now. I need to go."

She left for her home.

I stood there, still taking in the answer that I had just received. Those words stuck me as if bullets had just penetrated through my heart. My body felt heavy all of sudden. The life appeared to be crumbling in front of me. The thing that I had always dreamt of is the thing that I will never get. I had nothing left to live for. I had no reason to smile now. It felt as if my soul had left me and I was all alone in this body, which was now hollow from within. Tears rolled down my eyes. I cannot bear it anymore. I felt empty and had no reason to be alive anymore.

I looked at Vimal, who was paddling his cycle fast, to get to me. A wild thought came to my mind. I thought again about it and then I knew what I had to do.

Few seconds later, I was riding my cycle on the way that was not leading me to my home. Adrenaline and pain helped me paddle faster than my capacity. I paddled through the traffic. Vimal was right behind me, calling me out to stop, but instead of stopping, I kept on paddling.

I had something dangerous in my mind.

In few minutes, I was past Santram Temple and Mahagujarat Hospital. I still kept on paddling. I had no reason to stop now. Soon I was past Vaniyavad Circle and still paddling towards the Dharmsinh Desai University.

Few seconds later, the DDU campus appeared in front of me. I paddled harder. I thought of my decision again. I had never thought that I would have to face this. The thought that I will never get her bought tears in my eyes.

In the distance, I made out the bridge on the canal. I paddled towards it. My decision was final. There is no turning back now.

I was on the verge of the bridge. Few more paddles and I will be on the bridge. I turned my steering away from the bridge and kept on paddling.

This is how my life ends, I thought. I have nothing to gain in this world anymore. So why live in it.

I closed my eyes and saw her face smiling at me. A wide smile covered my face with tears in my eyes as I along with my bicycle dived into the water where my journey of life was about to end.

*

# CHAPTER 2
## Present Day

I opened my eyes and found myself underwater. To my astonishment, instead of struggling or choking for air, I was breathing. There was no sign of any marine life. The only thing my eyes could see was clear water all around me.

Then in the distance, I saw something move. I turned away from it to the opposite direction. From that direction too, I saw something move. I scanned all the direction and from all the direction, I saw something closing down on me.

I steadied myself in the water and waited for it to arrive. Slowly and steadily, it grew larger and larger and soon it had covered me from all the directions. It was some kind of smoke under water. It surrounded me on all sides and blocked my eyesight.

Few moments later, smoke disappeared in the same manner it had appeared. However, my surrounding was not the same any more. There was still no sign of marine life, but below me, on the floor, there was now a vast expanse of coral reef. Its beauty and breath-taking view took over my mind. Instead of questions like from where all of it had suddenly appeared or where I was, all that came to my mind was its astonishing beauty.

I swam towards it. Reaching there, I touched it. There was no response. Coral reefs were supposed to be home to many marine animals, but here, there was sign of none. I kept on poking the coral reef for any sign of living organism, but I found none.

I was about to swim away, when, all of a sudden, I felt a burning spot on my hand. I pulled my hand back. Yet the pain remained along with the burning. After few long moments of wait, my pain subsided. I was not sure whether if it had disappeared or my nerves had got used to it.

I looked at the coral that I had just touched. It was bright yellow-green in color with brown skeleton covering.

No. it was not a true coral. It was a Fire Coral. I had seen it on the Animal Planet. Although it looked a lot alike coral, it was part of Jellyfish and other stinging family.

I was lucky that my pain and burning caused because of touching the Fire Coral, had vanished. I had read that, the pain and burning feeling stayed for two days to two weeks.

Knowing of the dangers that I might face from this Fire Coral, I started swimming away from it and took precautions before touching any of the corals.

I kept on swimming until I noticed a movement in the corals from corner of my eyes. I searched for the source but failed to locate. I continued with my swim. Again, I saw something move. I stopped and focused on the ecosystem below me. Everything was still. No sign of any movement for a moment.

Then out of nowhere, a stripped snake emerged from the corals directly making its way towards me. It must have been 9 to 12 feet long. It swam effortlessly in the water towards me and I on the other hand remained steady.

It circled twice around me. I thought it would swim away but instead it directly moved to my neck and took a bite on my neck.

Surprisingly I did not felt any pain but why take any risk. I tried to shoo it away with my hands. I slapped twice on its body with my hand and in the end; it drifted away, disappearing in the corals.

My body felt no pain. No sign or symptoms of any poison effect. So finally believing that I was fine, I started swimming again.

This time from the distance, I saw a group of fish swimming towards me. From where I was, it appeared as if they were grey in color. I steadied myself in water and waited for them.

They got closer and closer.

Now I could see their features. Red eyes, red shade under their mouth, and shiny little teeth. Those teeth were much sharper for ordinary fish. Then I recognized those teeth.

No, it can't be. I started swimming away from the upcoming group of devils, the piranhas, but I was much slower than I had thought. Soon, they surrounded me.

Instead of attacking me, they swam past me but those who were close to me, grabbed a bite from my body. By the time, they all had gone there were many punctures in my body from which blood was bursting out.

I felt weakness taking over me so I started swimming up. I was half way up when all of a sudden; all of my senses gave away. I felt paralyzed. I tried to move my hand and legs but they disobeyed my commands. The only thing that I was able to move was my neck.

I was terrified. I could not feel my body in the water, and there were wounds all over, that were constantly letting blood out. I thought of the reason of this sudden disability, and then, it struck me.

It was the effect of the snakebite. I remember it now. The victim of sea snakes generally felt the symptoms after 30 to 40 minutes, and disability was one of them.

I cursed the snake for my situation and prayed the god for help, butinstead of help, god sent me death.

I saw a shark swimming towards me from the left. It must have been my blood because shark's smell senses are too good and they are by birth nocturnal hunters. I tried to move my hands and legs and swim away but my body parts did not respond. I tried to swim on my right by moving my neck on right repeatedly, but all that efforts were in vain. Moments later, I stopped my efforts of the horror that I was about to face.

From the right side, I saw a crocodile swimming towards me. There was no hope of escape now. I closed my eyes and let whatever may happen to me. I let my body float in the water.

I waited for pain from shark bite or from crocodile bite. However, it never came. Instead, it felt lighter on my right and left shoulder. I opened my eyes to see if they had really been there or I was just seeing the things, but what I saw was horrific.

The shark and crocodile were having my hands in their mouth. My hands, had been, separated from their sockets and no longer attached to my body. Both of the predators were taking their time of the treat.

I started crying. I do not want to die like this. I prayed to god to help me. I begged for the help. I begged him to save me, but again the help never came. Instead, my death got even worse. From the corals below, the snake that had bitten me was swimming towards me. In the distance, the Fire Coral was floating towards me. In addition to this, farther more, the group of Piranhas were coming back for me, and this time they were not alone. A big mummy Piranha, accompanied them to have a treat.

Snake being the closest arrived first. Immediately on its arrival, it started biting me on different body parts. Then was the turn of the Fire Coral. It floated to my back and stuck to my spine. I did not felt anything from both of them. However, seeing all of them in action horrified me.

Soon the Piranha party arrived and with its arrival, chunks off my body started disappearing. The mummy Piranha swam in circles around me as if examining his meal. She might be wondering which part of my body should be her first meal. I wished I was not here and wished it all to disappear, but that never happen. Instead, in a single grab, the mummy Piranha took off my head from my body and gulped it directly into the darkness of the void.

*

## CHAPTER 3
### Present Day, Vallabh Vidhyanagar

When I woke up and opened my eyes, I found my face covered in cake. I had barely opened my eyes when someone closed my eyes again and bunch of hands started beating me from all the directions.

"Happy Birthday...!" cried Aastha.

She is always first when it comes to wishing birthdays. After her, Vimal, Smit, Rajan, Visha, Minal, Dimpu, Brijesh, Jigar, Bhargav, Rohan, Brinda, Bhoomi, Nehal, and Shivani joined in to wish me my twenty-first birthday. After that, the boys took their time for treating me with birthday bums. Once they had their treat, they dropped me on the floor and took a seat at any place that they foundempty.

I tried to get up but my bums ached with the recent gift it had just received.

"It hurts! Idiots!" I complained.

"Yeah! We know!" Brijesh said. "There is no meaning in birthday bums without pain."

I was glowing red with anger and wanted to hit them all, but that was not going to happen. I was drastically outnumbered.

"Whatever!" I said instead.

"Aww! My baby's hurt." Shivani said. "Let me give you a hug."

She hugged me and all my pain was gone. She kissed me on the cheek and my face was red with a blush.

"Aww! My baby!" all the boys followed. They all hugged me from all the directions. Shivani had barely escaped their grip.

"Stop!" I shouted. "Leave me alone."

"No, my baby, no," Jigar said. "Let's get you a hug."

They kept their hold. The more I tried to get free, the more they tightened the grip. In the end, I stopped my efforts and they let me loose.

"That was fun." Rohan said.

"Yeah." Rajan joined in.

"Fun for you, not for me." I complained.

"Is that so?" Smit said. "Remember my birthday? When you all had your treat on me! This was the payback for that."

"Yeah!" I grinned. "That day was fun."

I helped myself up from the floor and sat on the chair near the table. We all had beaten each other on birthdays. It was kind of a custom now. Today, it was my turn. Next turn is of Vimal and then Smit again and so on.

After we had celebrated my birthday, sung birthday song, finished the cake, and washed my face, we sat there in peace and relaxed. On the next day, we were having the exams, of which, no one had a slightest of the worry. We were just focusing on the celebration right now. In background, we played the instrumental music from Hollywood movies. I held Shivani's hand in my hand and thought of the beautiful day that I was going to have.

Few moments later, girls had to leave for their rented room. Smit and Rohan had also gone out in the search of snacks and drinks. Brijesh and all other boys were busy with their cell phones. Seeing all busy, I went to the gallery and thought of the nightmare that I just had.

I was thinking of that when Vimal interrupted my thoughts.

"Same nightmare again?" He asked.

I nodded. He knew of that nightmare. I had that nightmare for so many times and whenever I had that nightmare, I had told him about it. No one else knew about it except for him. He knew more about me than I myself did. My secrets, my fears, my problems, my feelings, my sorrows, everything about me.

We stood there in silence. We had no idea what this nightmare meant. I was having the happiest days of my life. A month had passed since I had proposed to Shivani and she had said yes. Life was in full fun for me. We, all Sixteen of us, spent time together, hanging out at Gol-Gappa, which we referred as the Fort of the Sixteen. At college, at movies, at picnics, we were always together. My life was at its full and there was nothing missing in it. Joy, happiness, creativity, friends, enemies, I had everything in my life.

Everything.

Except for one. Parents.

I closed my eyes and remembered the day on which awful things of my life had started. Eight years have passed since that day but time

31

had failed to replenish the wounds in my heart. Above it, it had given me new wounds to live with. I still remember the day of proposal, when I had tried to end my life. I had wished that I had died on that day, saving me from more sufferings that was yet to come. However, that was not enough for me. Fate had stored still more wounds for me.

I do not know why Vimal had dived after me and saved me from drowning that day. I wish he had let me drown, but no, those sufferings were not enough for me. There was still more pain I had to face.

Later on that day, when my parents asked me about the reason behind me ending up in the canal with my bicycle, I had simply told them that I had lost control on the steering and it was just an accident. Not believing me, they asked Vimal. Thankfully, he stood by me on that day and told them, that it was an accident, which I had faced in a race. He never talked about it again to anyone, not even to my parents. I too never talked about it, and that was the biggest mistake I had made in my life.

After my first suicidal attempt, everything about me changed. I had made up my mind to end my life and always searched for a way to end it. I never talked to anyone. Not even with Vimal. Whenever he tried to make me feel good, I would start fighting with him to drive him away. I would shout on him to mind his own business and leave me alone, but he never did that. He stood by me even when I tried to send him away from me, and today, I feel so glad that he had stood by me during those fights. I never talked to him about Vaishavi and minded my own business. When I had moved to the boarding school, there also, I preferred being alone and talked to no one. I made no friends there and only companion that stayed with me was my loneliness.

In hostel, Vaishavi's smile haunted me, and I started missing the company of Vimal, who at hard times in my school had always comforted me. When burden of her memories got too much for me to bear, I would end up crying in bathroom. Sometimes, when I was too exhausted of crying, I slept in bathroom. When my warden had found me sleeping there for few times, he had called my parents to inform them of my behavior. On hearing such things from my warden, they had called me and asked, if I was fine. To that, I had always lied to them or avoided their questions and told them that I missed them. I never disclosed the truth to them and always heed it from them.

By the time I had finished my first year in the boarding school, I was already popular as weirdo in the school and my behavior no longer mattered to my warden. It was normal for him to find me sleeping in the bathroom. Somehow, I managed to pass exams, but in sports and curricular activities, I had still failed. My grades were of no concern to my parents. My parents were bothered about me and were wondering about the reason behind the change in their son in past one year. For me, the only thing that mattered was seeing that smile of her for one more time.

When the summer vacations came, I was dying to see her. The day I got back to the town, I directly went to her house. I found the doors locked and so disappointed, I returned to my home and locked myself in my room. Later on learning of my vacations, Vimal came to my house and told me that Vaishavi and her family had moved to London. He told me that he fought with her every day in the school. He had told her how I had tried to end my life and hated her for doing this to his best friend. Every time she came in front of him, he wanted to hit her. Knowing that his best friend was broken at heart because of her, he was never able to look at her without rage and anger surfacing on his face.

One day, she came up to him and asked him to forgive her, and gave him a letter, which she asked him to give it to me. She said this were her final words for me before she leaves for London. He said he will deliver the letter, but refused to forgive her. She accepted that and left.

The letter that he said was from Vaishavi, which I than opened said:

Dear Shiv,

It hurt me when I learned of your actions that you took after our talk. I did not want to upset you but I had no other option. My parents already foretell me as a life partner to someone. I cannot stand up against my parent's decision so I have to do this to you. I am sorry.

The things that you said to me that day were in no manner weird, strange, embarrassing, or anything but pleasant. Those were the most beautiful things that anyone had ever said to me. I am glad that you told me how you felt because I too felt the same for you. I do think I love you but I am bound to honor my parent's words and so what we want between us is what we cannot have.

I hope you will understand my situation and find someone else who is more in love with you than I am.

Yours,

Vaishavi

That day, I cried repeatedly. The girl whom I loved and the girl, who loved me, was gone forever. Vimal read the letter and told me that this was all a shit. He asked me to forget it all and move on; but how could I. It needs only a spark to light a fire, and these words of her were more than just spark to lighten a power in my love.

For whole vacation, Vimal and I kept ourselves locked in the room. We seldom came out. I would keep talking about her to him. I would tell him how I imagine her smiling; I would tell him how I want to take a dive in her dark brown eyes, and how I want to see her push a strand of hair behind her ears. All those things that reminded me of her, I would talk to him and to all that, he would just give a nod and say,

'this all is a shit!'

He wanted me to forget it all, and get going with my life, but my heart never wanted that to happen and kept my mind busy with her thoughts.

My parents kept worrying about me, but it was better for them to worry about me for such behavior than worrying about me for my suicide attempts. They kept on asking me for the reason behind such a behavior of mine, and every time they asked, I avoided answering them. Sometimes I will give in to their questions and cry in mother's arm but would not answer their questions. I kept it to myself. In the end, they stopped asking me any more questions and I no longer had to worry about answering them.

The next year in the boarding school was not as surprising as it had been earlier. The faces were familiar for me. Although I did not have any friend, I was no stranger there. For the first time, I missed my mother's arms where I had cried whenever I thought about Vaishavi. In addition, the worst part was that, I was seeing things now. Sometimes I saw her in the terrace, while sometimes I saw her seating beside me during lectures. Wherever I went, I saw her. In the beginning, only peaceful time for me was at night when I had somehow managed to sleep, but that too changed when I started having dreams of her.

Every single day, my life got more horrible than it was on the previous day. Every day just got worse than the earlier one and my life started feeling like that in the hell. In the end, when it was too much to bear for me, I took another grave step of my life. I tried another suicide attempt by intentionally sliding my leg from the stairs.

My attempt for death was in vain and I ended up in the hospital with minor fractures and injuries but nothing serious. Because of injuries, I was sent back home. Hostel authorities had told my parents that I had slipped my leg accidently but my mom knew me better. He asked me repeatedly if it really was an accident or I had done it on purpose. I told them repeatedly that it was an accident but she would not believe me. How could she? Her son had already faced death, twice, and he cannot risk her son any more. When I told her nothing was there to bother, she asked Vimal to get something out of me.

When Vimal asked me, I told him everything that was happening to me. He wanted me to tell everything to my mother. I refused to do so and asked him to keep it all to himself. He promised to keep it all to himself only if I would not do anything stupid to commit suicide again. I accepted his terms to keep my secrets safe. He did not believe me that I would not do anything stupid, and was always ready to tell my mother everything, if I showed even a minor hint of my stupidity. However, my behavior and mindset improved in his presence and I was starting to get out of trauma of my love life that had never begun.

Days passed by and I started recovering from the injuries. Then came the day when everything changed in my life, the day I will always remember, the day when my parents came to drop me to hostel. It was before they left that my mother called me in a corner.

"Promise me my son," she said. "…you will not do anything that will harm you."

I remained silent. I did not know where it had come from.

"I know this all are not accidents. You are trying to kill yourself. I do not know why but you are upset. You are broken. Whatever may be the reason you are hurting me in process. I am your mother, and you are my son and all that hurts you, hurts me, my son. I love you very much but you seem distant to me. I do not know why, or what is bothering you, the only thing I know is that my son is attempting suicide and it hurts me. I just want you to promise me. Promise me you would not do anything like that. Ever. Promise me, my son. Promise me."

Tears rolled down from her eyes. My heart melted away and my eyes gave away the burden of my heart. I hugged my mother and asked her to forgive me for my behavior.

"I promise you mom," I said. "I promise you that I will never do anything that will hurt you. I promise you mom. I promise you."

That day I smiled for the first time since the day of the proposal. I smiled for first time in two long years and it was a love of a mother that had bought smile back on my face.

"I'm sorry mother. It was just some feelings that had overtaken my heart that I forgot your love, but I promise that it will never happen again. I love you mother. I love you."

Later that night, late after they had left, I slept the most peaceful sleep I had ever slept in two years. Not only was my heart feeling light, I also felt special with all the love that I have discovered between my mom and me, but that too was for very short span of time.

Next day, my uncle came during school hours, picked me up from the school, and drove me to Nadiad. Instead of heading to home, he directly took me to crematory of the town. There, I saw two bodies covered in white cloth, ready for cremation. I asked my uncle of what was going on. I asked him of my parent's whereabouts, but all I got in response were tears that slid down his eyes.

I realized what was going on and what was this all about. My parents were on the logs of wood. The bodies ready for cremation were of my parents. For a moment, I stood there, shocked. Then realizing of what had happened, I ran to them and cried. I asked them to get up but they never did.

My uncle asked me to cremate my parent's body. I wanted to see their face for last time. They refused to do so because my parent's faces were beyond recognition. They said that because of the accident, every part of their body were beyond recognition. They identified the bodies on the base of the belongings of my parents. It was better for me if I do not see them in that condition and remember their beautiful image that they always had. I agreed and took a last glimpse of their physical existence before I cremated their body one after other.

For next twelve days, I stayed with my uncle and aunt. On the thirteenth day, I asked my uncle to take me to the hostel. He asked me if I would like to get away from boarding school. He could arrange my admission in previous school with my best friend, Vimal. I asked him not to do that and so he took me back to my hostel. He told me to contact him if I needed anything. I nodded, he left, and then I retired to my bed with my eyes letting out the pain that I held in my heart.

Days passed by and sometimes, I thought of committing suicide. Whenever that thought passed my mind, I heard the voice of my mother, asking me to promise not doing anything like that. I kept my promise and let those thoughts pass. I tried to merge up with other kids but failed to do so. I felt emptiness in me. I felt lonelier. Now I was all alone in this world. Although my uncle and aunt were nicer to me and tried to make me happy, I missed the love that I received from my parents.

Thus despite of all my efforts, I ended up being the same I had been the year before. Crying in bathroom, roaming alone, and not talking to anyone. I gave up my suicidal tendency to keep the promise that I had made to my mother. Instead, I started doing things that were dangerous to my life. I would catch snakes when everyone considered it too dangerous for anyone to catch. I had hoped that one of them would bite me, and this all would end but that never happened. All those snakes remained calm around me. With increase in incidents of the snake catches, everyone started considering me as the bravest boy around.

At the end, the year in the hostel passed all the same, it had the previous year, but everything I had felt the previous year, had doubled with the loss of my parents. Above it, as if things were not enough for me, I started having suicidal nightmares in which I saw myself committing suicide. Those dreams made my pain worse because in the nightmares I did what I had promised my mother that I would not do.

Later when I learned that dreams are just imaginations that came true, of the thoughts that you think during the day, I tried to solve the problem of nightmare. I started thinking of the positive things only and immediately switched to any other topic whenever I had any kind of thought of suicide. In the beginning, it was difficult for me but in the end, I won.

However, those nightmares just changed. Instead of suicides, anything would kill me in my dreams. In the nightmares, sometimes I see myself walking on the road and a car overruns me, or I am on a mountain and land gives away and I die in landslide, and such things. Only one thing was common in all those dreams and that was my death.

That was how I lived every day. Another year came by in hostel and it passed the same way it had for past two years, in pain and grief and nightmares. Because of this all, I passed out my SSC exams with very low results.

Again came next year. However, this year was not the same. It was because of Devanand Sir. He was new and was there for teaching painting. He came as Aamir Khan of Taare Zameen Par and I was his Darsheel Safary. Seeing me alone everywhere and noticing me as not much of a talkative boy, he asked me to participate in painting group that were developing paintings for an exhibition. I had first, hesitated to join but later decided to join on having nothing to do all the time.

Painting was new for me. The only thing that I had ever painted was few cartoons of Mickey Mouse; but that was no hurdle for Devanand. He was very good teacher and taught me how to make strokes. He taught me all other aspects and things that I needed for making good paintings. I learned those things and slowly and steadily, he carved out a fine painter from me. I started making paintings on canvas and paper with colors and pencils, but I found my hands best on the pencil. Therefore, I only made pencil sketches and left the color strokes for others.

I do not know why but all the paintings that I had later sketched were of animals that were in either pain or agony. Instead of painting something joyful in colors, mine were only pencil sketching in the shades of dark. All those paintings I had made it from my heart, expressed the pain that lay in my heart. I was glad that I learned the painting because it gave me a way to let out my pain. I was not alone now. Pencils and paper were my pals and I had them whenever I wanted to express something.

Apart from painting, Devanand sir also taught us the sport of soccer. Although he was not the coach, still he taught us the game. He was good at the sport, but soccer was not his main game. His main game was hockey in which he had been master in his days. He taught me the game and helped me in making my way to the school team. As days passed by, my reputation in the school improved because of my game and paintings.

The last two years were better than previous ones, or I may say best one in my life. I studied with my paintings and soccer game so my result had also improved. Now I had paintings and sports game to keep myself busy. My friend circle had developed with my soccer teammates and I was no more alone. I sometimes missed my Parents and Vaishavi but the strength of pain was not same as it had been earlier. Even my nightmares changed. The frequencies of its occurrences were less. Now the things that killed me in my nightmares were animals that I had painted. In my nightmares, I see paintings of animals that I had painted. I see that all of a sudden, the paintings get real and animal of the painting strikes on me and kill me. Still I enjoyed those days with my friend circle. They made me happy and I seldom missed my love and my parents.

Soon the good time ended. I passed out from the school with good marks and got admission in one of the college in Nadiad. I stopped painting and playing. I started being the same that I had been earlier. The pain and loneliness returned. So did the nightmares. Everything was same as it had been before two years. However, I was not alone in it now. My best friend, Vimal, had reunited with me. These three years of bachelors became the dark experience of my life, but with a brightness of friendship in it. I still had nightmares and seldom talked with anyone about it, except for Vimal. I tried painting again but could not focus on it. I tried joining the college team but there too, I could not focus on the game. It was as if something within me was holding me back. Despite of all my efforts I failed to blend in with other people and remained an outlier from all the clusters of the college.

After the bachelors came the masters and that was when my life changed. In the beginning, I was the same as I had been in bachelors, but later everything in my life changed, when I met Shivani.

In the masters, she was the first person to be my friend. Vimal noticed the change in me, and tried to patch a knot between us. I held myself back but my efforts were not of that strength as that of Vimal. Days passed by and our friend circle grew. We met Smit and Visha who was as irritating as Vimal. We started hanging out together and the fun began in our life. Slowly, the number of the best pals in my life, increased with arrival of Aastha and Dimpal. The lonely boy, who once had only one friend, was now discovering new fruits of friendships in form of Brijesh, Jigar, Rajan, Rohan, Minal, Nehal, Brinda, Bhargav and Bhoomi. All sixteen of us were always together. In picnics, in theatres, in class, wherever you see one, other fifteen follow behind.

As days passed by, Shivani and I got close to each other. I started feeling something for her and I told that to Vimal. I asked him to keep that to himself, but it was already too late for that. Everyone in our group, except for Shivani, knew about my feelings. Soon they started teasing me in her presence and absence.

Days passed by and one day, everyone convinced me to propose to her. We created a plan and schedule, to make it a special one and one month before my twenty-first birthday, I proposed her. She said yes and we were all celebrating my relationship with Shivani. After so many days, joy had returned to my life. I consistently had a nightmare, the same nightmare, repeatedly, but except for that, there was total joy in my life. Whenever I had that nightmare, I discussed it with Vimal and tried to sort out meaning behind it. We discussed and discussed, but never came to conclusion. In the end, we declared it as just ordinary nightmare, and stopped worrying about it.

Whenever I had that nightmare, I would think about it for a while and then forget. Today again, I was doing the same. I thought about what it was and what it meant. I was lost in my thoughts and trying to derive a conclusion of the nightmare, when Rohan and Smit called us in.

They had returned with cold drinks and chips. Everyone had taken their seat for the feast and if I delayed any further, chances of having anything left for me to eat was very less.

"Let's go!" Vimal said. "Or we won't have anything to eat."

I nodded and left for the feast leaving all of my thought behind to celebrate my day with my friends. My life was beautiful again and I was not going to miss even a single minute from it.

*

# CHAPTER 4

My birthday had started with absolute bliss. From 12:00 am onwards, I was showered with blessings and wishes from my friends and relatives. In the morning when I woke up, I still felt the gift on my bums that I had received at the night. Whenever I sat, I cursed them for the gift. I promised myself that I'll give them even more unpleasant birthday bums on their birthday. Anyways, apart for that part of my birthday, everything was pleasant and I was enjoying best day of my life.

I dressed myself in black shirt and blue denims in the morning. Then after, Smit, Vimal and I went to Shastri Maidan. There we relaxed ourselves on the ground and enjoyed the morning breeze. We talked and joked for a while and when we started feeling the heat from the sun, we left the ground.

We first went to Maharaja's Shop to have the morning tea and coffee and then left for our usual meeting place at Gol Gappa. That was where my birthday surprise was about to get revealed.

The moment I entered the Gol Gappa, my favorite song, Koi Tumsa Nahi from Krrish was played by the manager. As if that was not enough, Visha, Smit, Vimal, Aastha and all the others were lip-synching with the lyrics of the song. They had choreographed the song and were performing a stand-up dance to indicate that no one was like me. The way they did that, coordinating with the words in the song, my heart started overflowing with joy and all that joy was clearly visible to them from the tears on my eyes and smile on my face. This was the best surprise I could expect. I felt so special just because of them.

Once the song had finished, I walked to them and joined in where everyone started wishing me birthday wishes. Everyone was there for me. My classmates, my friends, girls whom I liked (that must have been Aastha's idea, I guess from the look that she had on her face when she caught me looking at them) and my uncle and aunt. In the center, on the table, was a cake that was decorated with rose buds.

All around the table, balloons were scattered on the floor, and on the right wall, along with other decorations, I saw 'Happy Birthday Shiv' decorated with flowers. My eyes didn't fail to register that everyone had dressed in white except for me. That bought a wide smile on my face.

I hugged everyone one after other and thanked them for this big surprise. It felt special to have such a surprise for a birthday.

Once I had met everyone, Shivani escorted me to the cake for the cake cutting ceremony. The moment I reached the cake, she started singing the birthday song in her melodious voice. Everyone joined in and started singing the birthday song. I blew the candles on the cake and started cutting it into pieces for everyone. One after other, everyone had their turn for the cake and then it was the time for the presents.

Everyone gave me cards and gifts wrapped in gift paper. One after other, I unwrapped the gifts and admired the gifts that I had received.

Once I had gone through all the gifts, I still had more gifts to explore which I had not yet received. Those were from my best friends.

First gifts were from Smit and Vimal. Smit gave me a box of poster colors and Vimal gave me a canvas. After handing over the gift to me, they took a pose in front of me and said...

"Now sketch us!"

Everyone laughed and so did I.

"Sure!" I said. "But not today..."

After that, it was Dimpal's turn. She gave me a memory card and asked me to insert it in my cell. I did what she had asked for. Once I was done, I opened up the file explorer to explore the contents of memory card. In it, I found collection of my favorite songs and music. I scrolled down and saw all of them. I smiled as I went through the songs, one after the other.

After Dimpal, it was Visha's turn. She handed over me a notebook.

"Is this a book full of advices?" I asked expecting the gift, on base of what I had always received from her in different situations.

"No!" she said. "It contains what you already know and had shared with others."

I wondered what it could be and when I opened it, I gasped in the air with the gift that I had received from her.

Every morning and night, I wished everyone good morning and good night, with a quote that randomly came into my mind, and to my surprise, Visha had written all those quotes into this book and presented it to me as a gift. That was one thoughtful gift.

After Visha's gift, it was Aastha's turn. When her turn came, she opened her bag and took out a thick scrapbook from it. The book was too thick for a scrapbook. She handed over the book to me.

"Open it!" she said.

I opened the book and smiled seeing the gift I had received from her.

Being the most photoholic in our group, she had gifted me the gift that suited her the most. The scrapbook contained photos of her and mine that were numbered and decorated. She had placed the photo in order, in which they were taken. The more I turned the pages, the more it showed how our friendship had evolved.

After that, I received few more gifts from my friends in their own way. One after other, I received gifts from all of them except for Shivani. She said her gift was special one and was meant only for me. Therefore, that gift was supposed to get unraveled only after everyone was gone.

Now, except for Shivani's surprise, there was nothing more left as a surprise for me. But that thought of mine got completely wrong, when, after the gifts session, Aastha went to manager and said something to him. In response, manager gave her the laptop. She turned the laptop on and started a video in it.

The video contained every single photo of mine from my birth that were snapped while I grew up. It also had some of the videos that my father had captured when I was a kid. By the time the 16 minutes and 38 seconds of video had completed its play, my eyes were completely wet. I missed my parents, but again I was glad that they had given me the gift of memories of my parents.

"Thank you! Thank you all." I said. "This is the best gift and the best birthday of my life. I don't know how to thank you all for this big surprise and gifts. But this is surely the best day of my life."

"We accept your gratitude, Mr. Shiv," Smit said. "But now let's move on to lunch. I feel hungry now."

"Okay! Let's go." I said.

"Hey! Wait!" Aastha said. "What about the photo session? No one had captured even a single snap of mine today."

Everyone laughed and to fulfill Aastha's command, we captured the snaps of my birthday.

After lunch, my uncle and aunt, and my classmates left for their respective home. Only sixteen of us were left behind. We kept all the gifts and presents at our room and went to the nearby theater for a movie. After two and a half hours of movie, we again came out and went to Shastri Maidan. We sat there and gossiped and joked. Soon, it started getting dark and Shivani signaled something to Aastha. After receiving the signal, Aastha stood up and said,

"It's getting dark, let's go."

"Yeah, let's get going." I said and was about to stand up, when Shivani pulled me down and said to others,

"Guys, we'll join you later at dinner. Till then give us some moments please."

"Okay, see you at dinner then." Aastha said.

"What okay?" Vimal said. "I am not going anywhere without Shiv."

"Give them privacy, you idiot!" Minal said, "This is boyfriend-girlfriend thing."

"It doesn't matter. He's my friend first and her boy-friend second."

"Try to understand, Vimal." I whispered to him. "Give us privacy."

"No, I'm not going anywhere without you. After all it's your birthday."

'Wow,' I thought. He doesn't want to leave me on my birthday.

"Understand man," I said again. "We need a moment alone."

"No," he said again. "I'm not leaving without you, unless you give me your wallet."

Oh! So this was his intentions after all then.

"I'm not giving you my wallet. Go now." I said.

"I'm not going anywhere. It's party time and I want your wallet."

"I'm not giving you anything." I said again.

"Okay then, I'm not leaving either"

He remained there while other started leaving. I plead to him to leave but he remained still.

"Nothing's gonna work until you give me your wallet." He said.

"Fine." I replied.

I took out my wallet from my pocket and handed it over to him.

"Take this and get lost." I said.

He grinned and left us alone.

"So, what's it?" I asked once he was completely gone.

49

"What's what?" She asked.

"The gift?" I said.

"Be patient, my boy," She said, "you will have it. Just be patient."

She then took out a gift-wrapped box from her purse and handed it over to me. I took it in my hand and unwrapped the gift cover from it. It was a velvet box, with our names engraved on it in a heart shape. I opened the box and took out a wristwatch from it.

"That's it?" I asked. "You bought me a wrist watch. That is all you have. You could have given this to me with other gifts. Why make me wait this long?"

"You sure lack patience." She said. "Now shut your mouth and wear this on your hand."

I did as I was told. I wore the wristwatch on my wrist and showed it to her. She pointed her finger at the watch.

"What?" I asked. "It's 6:45 after noon. That's right time."

She took my hand in her hand and turned the pendant of the watch in clockwise direction.

"Okay, now?" she asked.

I looked at the pendant and was surprised to see what I saw in the watch. Instead of clock showing the time, there was a picture of her and mine.

"How did you do that?" I asked her.

She again turned the pendant back, anti-clockwise and the clock with the time was back.

"This is amazing." I said and turned the watch pendant myself.

"How did you made this?" I asked her, still not believing the amazing gift that she had given me.

"Nothing's hard if you know right words for searching mechanics in internet." She said.

"Still, this is so amazing." I said.

I looked at the photo that was there in the wristwatch. At first, I thought, it was just a photo that she had pasted in it with a glue, but when I looked at it carefully, I realized of what it actually was.

"You painted that?" I asked her.

"Yes." She said. "Do you like it?"

"Like it? My god this is amazing. I had no idea that you could paint so well. The details, the strokes, I thought it was a photo."

"I am glad that you liked it." She said.

I held her hand in mine and looked at her eyes. Then I kissed her on the cheek and said,

"Thank you for this wonderful and mechanical gift. I don't have words to describe how lucky I feel to have you in my life."

She smiled and gave me a hug.

"I know." She said. "You are one lucky guy to have me."

We both laughed at that and remained there for a while. We held each other's hands and enjoyed the most romantic moments of our life. Soon, it was dark enough and it was time for us to leave. We stood up, left the ground, and started walking towards my bike.

This was the best birthday of my life. There was still few moments of that special day left with me and I was going to enjoy it with best people in my life. There is nothing better in this world than few precious moments with true love and true friends. I again looked at the wristwatch and thought of how lucky I was to have these people in my life. After that, I started my bike and left for the grand dinner that we were about to have for my birthday.

*

# CHAPTER 5
## Junagadh

A month after my birthday, all sixteen of us were on our way to Gir National Park. Our exams had completed and it was time for us to enjoy. We had planned a trip to Gir National park, together, to enjoy the break.

Situated at the foothills of Mount Girnar, Junagadh was one of the places on the earth that offered the chance to probe the earth and the heavens, the human and the wild at same time. The city is the seventh largest in Gujarat and was located southwest of state capital Gandhinagar and Ahmedabad.

We had left at around 4:00 PM after noon, in a rented Cruiser and had reached the city of Junagadh at 7:30 PM. We felt the change as soon as we had seen the hills of Junagadh. The atmosphere here was much better than that of any other city. The air was clean and there was greenery everywhere. The weather here was cool and peaceful.

I had seen Lions but only in zoo at Sayaji Bagh in Vadodara. However, seeing the king in its own realm holds its own thrill. I had always wanted to visit the jungles with my parents when I was child, but those wishes never came true and now it never will. Anyway, now was my chance to fulfil my wishes of wild with my friends. I had already seen Tigers, on my last trip at Kanha National Park in Madhya Pradesh and now, it was turn for Asiatic Lions at Gir National Park. Next year, maybe, we might plan a trip for Rhinos at Kaziranga National Park.

All the time during our ride to the city, everyone joked and played games. We played Antakshri and Dum-Sararas and Guess-My-Name games. At time when everyone was tired and asleep, Shivani and I had shared our moments of romance. I held her hands in mine and laid down my head in her lap. We talked and talked and talked until everyone hade woke up again. Again, the fun began when we sang songs and mimicked our college professor's expressions. We talked about movies and argued on who was better than whom. We ate snack, drank drinks, snapped memories in photos and did all the stupid things possible in a vehicle.

When the brakes of the Cruiser screeched, we were in front of the Leo Resorts. We had booked four rooms for ourselves. Two for girls and two for boys. After unloading the baggage from the Cruiser, we checked into our respective rooms. Smit, Vimal, Brijesh and I had taken the one, while remaining boys had occupied the other. In same manner, girls divided themselves in two groups for two rooms. Once we had all freshen up and felt energetic enough to start our tour, we left for the dinner.

It was already dark when we came out of the resort for the dinner. We had planned to have our dinner at food stalls in the market instead of the resort. We ate Punjabi and drank Masala-Chaas followed by desert of Chocolate Cones at nearby ice cream parlor. After that, we went for the trip of the local market. At around eleven, we agreed to get back to the resort. My head was feeling heavy and I was in no mood for any more trip. So seeing my condition, we made back to the resort, where, girls retired for the night to their room and four of us, Brijesh, Smit, Vimal and Me, retired to ours.

In the resort room, I had nothing to do but give up to the headache that I had in my head. I had no other option but to lie down on the bed. I switched on the air conditioner and let my mind loose. Slowly, I drifted away to sleep while romantic thoughts of my love Shivani, kept my mind busy.

*

In the morning, I sat on the chair watching the television. Vimal was in bathroom and Smit and Brijesh were still in the bed. I had already tried to wake them up, thrice, but they had remained asleep and not even opened their eyes once.

Half an hour later, Smit got up from the bed and proceeded towards the bathroom. By that time, Vimal was already ready. After another half hour, Brijesh followed behind while Smit was getting ready. Half an hour later, he came out and within few minutes, got dressed. From there, we left for other boys and from there, to the girls. Once we all were fresh and ready, all sixteen of us left for the breakfast.

After completing our breakfast, we started with our tour from Upperkot Fort.

"We forgot to hire a Guide." I said as we stood there in front of the fort.

"We didn't." Smit Said.

"Just watch on." Rajan added.

We started walking towards the fort. All of a sudden Smit stopped. He held his mobile in one hand and with other hand showed the fort to us as if he was our instructor.

"Upperkot Fort was originally built during the Mauryan dynasty by Chandragupta Maurya in 319 BC...", he started "...and since then it has been rebuilt and extended many times over the centuries. The fort remained in use until the 6th century, when, it was been left abandoned for some 300 years, and again rediscovered in 976 CE. The fort had besieged 16 times over a 1000-year period. One unsuccessful siege had lasted for twelve long years."

He looked at us with smile.

"How was that?" He asked.

"That's too much to remember." Dimpu said.

"Obviously it is!" Visha said. "If not, then wouldn't we all be the guide!"

"Why worry when we got Wikipedia and Google with us." Rajan said.

We walked to the fort and took in the surrounding area.

"It is also said that..." Rajan started this time. "...the fort was abandoned from the 7th to 10th centuries and, when rediscovered, was completely overgrown by jungle."

We entered the fort whose entrance formed an ornate triple gateway. This gateway was like the Hindu Toran, leading to flat land dotted with various archeological sites. In some of the places, the walls of fort were as high as seventy feet.

We walked in the fort. We started examining and capturing the snaps of the fort while Smit and Rajan were busy with their instructor thing. The fort had many interesting exhibits. One of them was canon guns, placed on the western walls of the fort.

"For your information..." Smit continued with the guide thing,

"…these canons are believed to be have cast in Egypt. Wikipedia also says that Upperkot Fort had two-step wells - Adi-Kadi Vav and Navghan Kuva, a tomb, mosque and some ancient Buddhist caves belonging to 200 BC to 200 AD, which were located within the fort premises. Now only, some of the ruins of the buildings, Jama Masjid and the Buddhist caves are located within the fort premises."

We observed the surroundings and tried to relate it to what our guide was narrating about it. After few minutes we reached to the Adi-Kadi Vav and Navghan Kuvo, the two step wells, which were located within the fort.

We looked in the water and took some snaps of it. As earlier, Smit and Rajan were busy with their instructor role of reading out the information.

"These wells were built by the Chudasama Rajputs and are the unique water structures among the various step wells of Gujarat." He said.

"Both these wells served as the main sources of drinking water for years and were the essential part of the basic need of the fort. The Adi-Kadi Vav has a long flight of 120 steps, built in the 15th century, which lead to the water. While the Navghan Kuvo was built in 1026 AD from soft rock and is 52 meter deep, reached by a circular staircase winding around the shaft."

After the wells, we got out in open and took in the view of the city and east of Girnar Hill. The views from here were superb.

From there, we went to Jama Masjid, the mosque inside the fort that was converted from a palace in the 15th century by Sultan Mahmud Begada. It had a rare roofed courtyard with three octagonal openings, which I suppose, once, had been covered by domes.

From there we went to Buddhist caves. This were not actually caves but monastic quarters carved out of the rock about 2000 years ago. The three-storey complex is quite eerie and the main hall contains pillars with weathered carvings.

After that, we left the Fort and made our way to Durbar Hall Museum. Durbar Hall Museum houses a large collection of silver chains, chandeliers, thrones, palanquins, weapons and armor from the days of the Nawabs. There is also a portrait gallery of the Nawabs. This museum was once the hall where the Nawabs held their Darbars.

After seeing the exhibits at the museum, we left for our next stop, which was Mahabat Maqbara. It is a stunning mausoleum of one of the Nawabs of Junagadh. Built in 1892 and topped with silver doors and intricate architecture, including minarets encircled by spiraling stairways, this mausoleum is one of the Gujarat's most glorious examples of Indo-Islamic architecture.

After seeing Mahabat Maqbara, we left for Girnar Hills. On the way, we stopped at Ashoka's Rock Edicts, which are located on the route to the Mount Girnar hill. This rock edict is a huge boulder housed in a small roadside building. On the rock edicts, the fourteen Edicts of Emperor Ashoka are inscribed. The inscriptions carry Brahmi script in Pali language and belongs to 250 BC. On the same rock, the inscriptions in the Sanskrit language are also inscribed. The Ashoka's Rock Edicts incorporate moral lectures. The emperor Ashoka began the stone writing history of Junagadh on this boulder. His 14 edicts in Pali states that he, the Beloved of the Gods, looks after all his subjects.

After the Ashoka's Rock Edicts, we took a break for lunch, and from there, we would continue with our tour to next destination, Mount Girnar.

Mount Girnar is one of the hill in Girnar Hills, which is most sacred to the Jain community. This hill rises to a height of more than six hundredmeters, a climb marked by ten-thousand stone-steps. On this hill, various Hindu and Jain temples are located. There is a group of sixteen Jain temples on the hill. Millions of Hindus and Jains visit this sacred hill, every year. At the top is the Amba Mata temple, which is, visited by the newlyweds in order to ensure a happy marriage. One of the largest and the oldest Jain temple, dedicated to the Neminath, the Twenty second Jain Tirthankar, and the Mallinath, the nineteenth Jain Tirthankar, are located, below the Amba Mata temple. Built in twelfth century, there is an image of Neminath in each of the courtyard colonnade's seventy cells. The corbelled domes, maidens and flying figures as decoration are typical of the Solanki period. During the Kartika Purnima festival in November and December, a very popular fair takes place here. Besides this, the Bhavnath temple of Hindus, dedicated to the Lord Shiva, is also located on this hill. Naga Sadhus and pilgrims from all over India attend the Mahashivaratri fair held here. Once a traveler to Gujarat, Joss Graham, climbed up the hill for the festival of Shivaratri, and slept there overnight. He woke up on hearing the praying murmurs of the great mass of devotees, about one lakh of them in their communities and tribal groups. There is also the temple of Samprati Raja, a fine example of the later period and the Melak Vasahi temple.

At 2:15 PM, we started with our pilgrimage of Mount Girnar. We passed the entrance gate and reached to the stairs. From there we started the climb of ten thousand stairs.

We started with Darshan of Lord Hanuman, Amba Mata and Lord Dattatreya at foothills. It was from there that our actual pilgrimage of the Mount Girnar, started.

We had hardly passed two hundred steps and our breathing got heavy. Few more hundred steps and our breath got heavier. The breeze was starting to get cool now.

"Is it compulsory to go?" Shivani asked breathing heavily. She was all red.

"It is!" Aastha replied. "It will be shame if you go back home, without climbing Girnar, when you are on a tour of Junagadh."

Shivani gave her an evil eye. I took her hand in mine and started the climb.

Earlier I had heard about Girnar climbing from many people. Whenever they said that it was hard to climb the hill, I had thought that it was a child's play to climb hills. However now, I realized that climbing mountains or hills are not as easy as it sounds.

At eight hundredth step, Shivani and I, stopped and sat there on the step. Smit and Dimpu too stopped and took place beside us.

"We should return back." I said to them. "We won't make it to the top."

"Is that all you got, hmm." Vimal said. "You today's youths haven't got stamina at all. Now stop complaining and keep climbing."

"Yeah, yeah. Whatever." I said.

Then at one-thousandth step, we hired walking sticks for thirty rupees, which later proved more helpful in the climb.

By the time, we had reached two-thousandth step we were soaking with perspiration and our faces were expression less. We had just climbed one-fourth of the path and already felt tired of the climb. We sat there and relaxed ourselves, feeling the cool breeze and taking in the view of Dataar Hills in front of us.

After few minutes of rest, we continued with our climb. On the way, we met many other people who had given up climbing the hill. They asked for forgiveness to Lord Dattatray and Goddess Amba for not making it to their temples.

From three-thousandth step, we had breath-taking view of Girnar Taleti and Junagadh City. With every step, view below us got more and more beautiful. However, the beauty before us was still not enough to overrun my thoughts. Only thoughts that came to my mind was that of reaching the top and then taking rest for a while.

After four thousand and five hundred steps of climbing, we reached to the Tirthankara Neminath temple. Although there were many Jain temples on Mount Girnar, Tirthankara Neminath temple is most important of them.

According to Jain religious beliefs, Neminath, the twenty-second Tirthankar became an ascetic after he saw the slaughter of animals for food on his wedding. He renounced all worldly pleasures and came to Mount Girnar to attain salvation. Here, Lord Neminath reached the highest state of enlightenment, Keval Gyan and Moksha, after great austerities. His bride-to-be also followed his path and founded the Sadhvi Sangh, the organization of women ascetics.

The rectangular Neminath temple has an idol of Lord Neminath in black granite with jeweled eyes. There are quadrangle courtyards, corridors and other shrines. The pillars have adorned with intricate carvings of Jain Tirthankars. The ceilings bear carvings and sculptures of Dancing Goddesses. It is believed that the twenty-second Tirthankara Neminath had died on Mount Girnar after seven hundred years of meditation and asceticism is depicted as a black figure sitting in the lotus position holding a conch in the marble Neminath Temple.

Once we had visited the Jain temple, we visited nearby food stalls. From here, we purchased the water bottle at thrice of its original value. Tourist had no other choice but to pay the amount because no other place provided water bottle at top of the hill.

After taking the rest of few minutes, we resumed our journey towards Goddess Amba's temple. This is one of the very ancient temples of India. Goddess Amba's Temple is highly sublime pilgrimage center for the Hindus. Amba Mata Temple attracts more than lakhs of pilgrims from all parts of the world, throughout the year.

Dedicated to an incarnation of the mother Goddess Ambaji, the main visitors of the temple are newly wedded couples. They come here to acquire the blessings of the Goddess Amba Maa and secure the eternal conjugal bliss.

The deities of pre-Aryan race, mostly worships Goddess Amba. In this mountain, one can find imprinted footsteps of Goddess. There are also imprints of her chariot, which were here, even before the construction of the Amba Mata Temple. According to legends about the temple, the tonsure ceremony of Lord Krishna did take place in this religious site. A Golden Yantra exist in the Amba Mata Temple with fifty-one 'shlokas' on it and in the courtyard of the temple premises, the folk drama called 'Bhavai', is performed.

After climbing six-thousand steps, we reached the Goddess Amba's Temple and there joined the queue of two-hundred other pilgrims who were standing there for the darshan of the Goddess. After standing in the queue for few minutes, we gave up the idea of waiting and decided to visit the temple on our return journey.

Therefore, from there, we started our climb for Guru Gorakhnath Temple. Guru Gorakhnath was an eleventh to twelfth century hindu nath yogi, connected to Shivaism and was one of the two most important disciples of Guru Matsyendranath. The Nath Tradition underwent its greatest expansion during the time of Gorakhnath. In his life, he did lot of miracles just to teach real spiritualism and bhakti.

Upon the sacred height of Girnar, there are many temples. The hill consists of five principal peaks, the highest of which, with an altitude of three thousand six hundred and sixty six feet, is associated with the name of Gorakhnath. Above the shrine of Amba Mata there is another three feet square, dedicated to the great disciple of Guru Matsyendranath. It is said that Goddess Parvati, in search of Lord Shiva, dwelt at Girnar, and that she continued to sing the praises of her Lord, until at this spot, he finally showed himself to her. In the legends, representation of Girnar is of a noted place of resort and a favorite haunt of Gorakhnath. He used to stay here and his dhuni still exists.

After climb of few minutes, we reached to the dhuni of Lord Gorakhnath and from there we visited the actual place where Guru Gorakhnath used to Meditate. Today at that place, there is a small temple with an idol of Guru Gorakhnath.

From Guru Gorakhnath Temple, Lord Dattatreya Temple was clearly visible; however, we failed to locate any path that could take us to the temple. After searching for the path, we finally saw the steps leading down and realized that we will have to climb all the way down and from there up again to reach the Lord Dattatreya Temple. In addition, we had to circle whole hill to reach the temple, which made the journey even longer.

Lord Dattatreya or Datta is a deity encompassing the trinity of Brahma, Vishnu and Shiva, collectively known as Trimurti. In the Nath tradition, Lord Dattatreya is recognized as an incarnation of Shiva and as the Adi-Guru (First Teacher) of the Adinath Sampradaya of the Nathas.

Dattatreya was born to the sage Atri, who was given the boon by Parameshwar that he, Parameshwar, will incarnate as his son. Since Parameshwar subsumes all three members of the Trimurti, Dattatreya is at once the incarnation of Vishnu, Shiva and Brahma.

Datta left home at an early age to wander in search of the Absolute Truth. He seems to have spent most of his life wandering in the area between and including Karnataka, Maharashtra and Andhra Pradesh, and into Gujarat as far as the Narmada River. He attained realization at a town called Ganagapura in Karnataka. The original footprints of Datta are believed to be located on the lonely peak at Girnar and that peak was the one on which we stood right now.

After climbing two-thousand steps down and again eighteen-hundred steps up again, we reached the Temple of Lord Dattatreya. Instead of visiting the temple, we sat there and relaxed for a while. After few minutes, we entered the temple. There we prayed to Lord Dattatreya and received blessings from the Pujari. We took prasad from him and started our way out of the temple. On the way out, I was fighting with Smit and Vimal for the prasad and trying to grab the prasad from one other's share when I accidently broke an old jar placed near the door.

Hearing the sound of breaking jar, Pujari turned and came to me. By that time Smit and Vimal had already left the temple, so had everyone else, leaving me behind in the situation that I will have to handle on my own.

"Umm, sorry Pujariji," I apologized, expecting a scolding lecture from him. "I had no intention of breaking it. It happened accidentally."

"Accidentally or not, you have to pay for it now." He said.

"I'm ready for it. How much did it cost?" I asked taking out the wallet from my pocket.

"Money can't buy everything, my son!" Panditji said.

"Then how am I supposed to pay? Panditji?"

"You'll have to wear this thread."

I looked at him quizzically as he pulled out a red thread from the white sand, which had poured out of the broken jar. I had expected some punishment like donating some money or something like that but this was unexpected. I gave him my hand to tie the thread.

"I had waited very long for this jar to break." He said while tying the thread. "And finally it has. Thank god, I had lived long enough to see it in pieces. May god bless you my son and protect you from upcoming dangers."

"Excuse me but I'm not getting anything of what you are talking about." I said.

"You will once the time is due. Your journey has just begun and you are going to face a very tough time. If you survive through, you will meet the immortal king whom I had always wanted to see."

"What journey? Which king?" I asked him.

"Time will answer that. For now, take this another thread and give it to the one that you want to protect, to one for whom you care."

He took out another thread with a Rudraksh from the sand, and tied it above the thread that he had just tied.

I looked at the Rudraksh and wondered what was this all about. I again looked at the Panditji, but he was already busy with his pooja dish.

I left the Lord Dattatreya Temple. Outside, everyone was waiting for me.

"What happened? Got a scolding?" Vimal said with a big grin.

He was expecting it to be a chance for him to make fun of me.

65

However, this time, I had upper hand on him.

"Nope! Not Actually! Panditji gave me more prasad and even gave me this thread as a blessing!" I said pointing to the threads on my wrist.

"What? Is he gone crazy? He should have scolded you for breaking that jar! It must have been there for years and you broke it? He must have scolded you! You must be lying."

"But he didn't! And I even got more prasad!" I said with a big grin.

This time I had it. Therefore, instead of saying anything more, he turned around and started walking. Smit and I laughed at him for we knew food was Vimal's weakness and this time I had him.

Anyways, after that, we were on our way back and soon, had reached to Lord Gorakhnath's Temple. By that time, we were relieved that we were past the quota of upward climb. Rest of our journey was climbing down which was much smoother and less tiring task than climbing up. We started the journey down and soon reached to the final stop of our Journey.

By the time we had reached Goddess Amba's Temple, the queue had disappeared and so we got our turn quickly and peacefully.

After finishing the Darshan at Goddess Amba's temple, we resumed our journey and this time there was no stop on the way.

After an hour and a half of downward climb, we had reached the main entrance gate but instead of feeling tired of the journey, we felt energetic. We took our dinner at the foothills and after completing the dinner, we headed back to the resort.

Once back to the resort, effect of the journey took over us and soon we fell our legs aching. I along with Vimal used the bed to spread ourselves, whereas Smit had used the stool to spread his legs and had turned on the television. Brijesh was out in the market with Jigar and was not coming back for a while. Shivani and I had planned a romantic walk after the trip, but the tiredness had forced us to cancel the plan. Thinking about our romantic days, soon I lost myself in a peaceful sleep while wondering about how, I was going to continue our romance on next day.

*

# CHAPTER 6

Next Morning, I sat on my bed, flipping through the channels on television. Vimal was again in bathroom and Smit and Brijesh were again on bed. It was 8:15 in morning and I was trying to pass the time. As I tried to focus on the television, my mind drifted back to the thread on my wrist.

Pujari's words were playing in my mind. I had no idea of what it was that he was talking about at that time, but whatever it was, his words were playing in my head again and again like a recorder set on a repeat mode.

Few minutes later, Vimal emerged out of the bathroom. He had covered his lower body with towel and his upper body was still dripping with water.

"Got everything ready buddy?" he asked.

"Yeah." I replied.

Fifteen minutes later, Smit went to bathroom and then Brijesh and another hour later, we were out to continue with the tour.

We had joined a safari tour of Gir National Park, which will take tour of half of the part of National Park today and remaining half of the park on the next day. The safari starts from Sasan Gir; the headquarters of the Gir National Park and Gir Sanctuary.

The safari was supposed to have three separate timings from morning to evening with two intervals. However, with help of bribe, we had combined three timings of safari into two with only one break to spend more time in the forest. One can hire an open Gypsy, which is very thrilling and thoroughly recommended.

I had prepared my camera for the tour with few extra batteries and a bottle of water to drink during the tour, and wallet having few thousands in it for snacks and stuff. I had not bought the wristwatch that I had received from Shivani, on the tour to keep it safe from any kind of damage.

At the gate, we sat on the bench waiting for the safari Jeeps to arrive. After few minutes of wait, we spotted three Jeeps driving towards us.

All the Jeeps stopped in front of us. A man ran to us from the first Jeep!

"Shiv and group?" he asked.

"Yes." I said.

"Welcome sir, I'm Yogendra Rajput, the tour organizer." He said. "This will be your Jeeps for two-day safari. If you need anything or have any problem during the tour, you can contact me. Anything you would like to ask?"

"Nope." I replied.

He returned to his Jeep and we divided ourselves in three Jeeps. Each Jeep had five occupants except for ours. Smit, Vimal, Shivani, Aastha,

Visha and I had occupied the first Jeep. Brijesh, Rohan, NehaI, Dimpu and Jigar were in second and all other left, had occupied the third one. As we settled in the Jeep, engines roared to life and soon we were on our way to Gir National Park.

We drove through the city towards the jungle. As we got close to the jungle, we saw boards and hoardings, which indicated that Gir was the only place in the world having Asiatic lions. Some hoardings asked to stop civilization in their area, and some asked to catch the poachers poaching the lions. Those were the posters from environmentalists, who were fighting against the civilizations and deforestation on the land of the beasts.

After fifteen minutes of drive in fun and mischiefs between us, we saw the gate to the national park. On the way, Bhargav's Jeep overtook ours and was at first followed by our Jeep and then Jigar's.

At the entrance, we saw never ending queue of Gypsys and Jeeps that were waiting for their turn to enter the national park. As we got close, we got clear view of the gate and things beyond it. In the distance, there was another gate within the boundary. In between them was a huge cage, kept very next to the inner gate.

"Scared?" I asked Shivani.

"No!" She said. "Excited."

I smiled at her. Smit and Vimal nudged me while Shivani was having the same from Visha and Aastha. Everyone knew it from my face that I was blushing heavily.

Slowly and steadily, we got closer and closer to the entrance as the vehicles that had arrived before us,entered the park. When first Jeep of our tour group reached the gate booth, three men approached each of our Jeeps.

The man that approached us was having boyish features with thin body and dark color hair.

"Hi everyone," he said. "I'll be your safari guide for today and tomorrow. I am Bhanu Pratap Singh and you can call me Bhanu. I'll be back in minutes after getting your tickets."

After introducing himself, he left again towards the entrance post. He gave us the tickets of safari, which tour organizer had already charged in our tour package. Again, he left us for completing the entry process, and after few moments returned back.

"What is that cage for?" Vimal asked.

"That cage contains a lion. Sometimes, tourists don't get to see a lion. Therefore, forest authorities have kept this cage at the entrance so that none of the tourists returns without seeing the Asiatic Lion. And if you haven't spotted any Lions in your safari than you could always visit the interpretation zone, Dewalia Park, where lions were kept within fenced boundaries of their natural environment, unlike the open jungles of the national park."

We passed the entrance terminal and again joined the queue inside for entering the Gir forest. From the queue, we got clear view of the cage now. It had only one lion, which was sleeping on the other end of the cage.

I took out my camera and turned off the flash. Then I started capturing the photos of the sleeping king.

Meanwhile, a kid from a Gypsy behind us was struggling to catch a glimpse of the lion. Beast being at the other corner was not visible to him. He climbed on the seats to see the lion. As he got clear image he saw that the lion was sleeping. In order to wake the beast up, he threw his toy lion towards the sleeping beast.

The toy glided through the air towards the sleeping king and struck the beast on its head awakening him from his peaceful sleep.

Lion, awakened from the sleep, lost his temper. He got up from his place and started running towards the jeep that carried the kid. As he ran for the Gypsy, he focused his sight on the kid and started the run in full throttle. As he came closer his size grew and grew, until he was big enough in size and had banged with the cage grill. Because of the clash, the cage grill shivered and everyone in nearby vehicles fell down with sudden outrage of the beast. Every Jeep passenger had his or her eyes focused on the cage now.

Meanwhile one of the guard, who saw these events, ran inside the check post room and brought out the gun.

At same time, irritated of having bars between him and his prey, the king of the forest retreated few steps and again smashed his body with the bars with even more power this time.

After that, we heard a shot as a bullet struck the beast on his shoulder. As a result, he got more furious and started retreating again to collide with more power. However, before his body could meet the grill, another bullet pierced through his skin. As a result, he lost his conscious, skidded towards the cage, and banged with the grill with a low thud.

Shocked with the sudden shift of events we got up one after other, and stood their paralyzed. The boy was terrified and tears rolled down his eyes. Aastha held herself to Visha, fear clearly visible on her face. I held Shivani in my arms as things around us got under control.

I searched for my camera that I had lost during the incident. I searched it in the jeep and failed. There was no sign of it.

"It's there!" Vimal said, pointing at the camera on the dirt road.

I peeped out of the jeep and there it was on the dirt road next to the Jeep's wheel, turned on with its lens towards the cage.

Before I can jump out of the vehicle to get my camera, a man with well build body and baldhead, picked it up and gave it to me.

I don't know how, maybe by hitting the ground, my camera had switched to recording mode and as I went through it I found that it had recorded whole incident after the first bang.

"He isn't dead. Just out of conscious." said the man staring at the lion who was lying unconscious in the cage. Slowly he walked to the kid's jeep.

"We don't kill them. They are precious and endangered." He continued and then faced us.

"You all were lucky that there was the grill protecting you all from the beast. Or else you all would have died before you had even realized, what hit you."

He paused for a moment and then continued.

"It was your fault." He said pointing towards the guide of the kid's gypsy.

"You should have given them the instructions. I want you to meet me in my cabin after the trip."

I do not know why he thought it was guide's fault. His job of guiding starts after entering the main gate and even though if it was duty of guide, there was no way he could have stopped that stupid kid from throwing the lion toy.

"…and I'm sorry to say that this kid cannot join the safari." he said pointing towards the kid.

Moments later, we resumed the journey. As time passed one after other, every vehicle passed main entrance and at last, it was our turn to pass. Once, the check post guard had thoroughly checked and performed other formalities, they allowed us to enter the park, accompanied by an armed guard.

"Okay then." Our guide started. "We will be exploring the jungle from here and before we do, there are the rules that must be followed strictly. First, you are not supposed to harass any animal. This time, there will be no bars. Secondly, do not throw wrappers, any plastic, or any type of material in the forest. It may kill animals if they consume it. Thirdly switch off the flash of the camera. Fourthly, none of you is supposed to leave the vehicle in any circumstances. And finally never make a noise in a presence of an animal."

By the time the guide completed the instructions the entrance gate was a small dot in the distance. As we travelled on the dirt road, leaving the civilization behind, we got the feeling of change in the surrounding.

Even though the atmosphere and everything was same, there was feeling of wilderness. After few straight kilometers in the park, we reached a point where the road lead to two different paths, of which; one was going on the left and other on the right. We continued the drive with the road on the left.

"Today we will be taking route two and six on which lions are spotted the most." Said the guide. "Now let me tell you something about Gir. Gir, known all over the world as the last home of the Asiatic lion, is the only place in India and whole world where you can find Asiatic Lions. The lions were once widely distributed in Asia Minor and Arabia through Persia to India. In the Indian sub-continent, its range extended over northern India, as far as east up to Bihar, with the Narmada River marking the southern limit. Before the close of the last century, the Asiatic lion had become extinct from its range except

.

Gir. The probable years of its extermination were Bihar in 1840, Delhi in 1834, Bhavalpur in 1842, Eastern Vindhyas & Bundelkhand in 1865, Central India & Rajasthan in 1870 and Western Aravallis in 1880. The last animal surviving in the wild outside Saurashtra was in 1884.

By the end of the last century, the then Nawab of Junagadh indicated the number of lion to be a dozen in the Gir. Lions struggled to survive during one of the most severe famines between the years 1901 to 1905 as they killed many human beings and domestic cattle. The Nawab of Junagadh provided adequate protection to the animals, and hence, the population of lion increased between the years 1904 to 1911. After the death of the Nawab, there was hunting of around twelve to thirteen lions, every year. From the year 1911 onwards, the British Administration rigidly controlled shooting and during the year 1913, the Chief Forest Officer of Junagadh reported that there were not more than twenty animals in the Gir Forest. Later, with help of better administration and strict laws, the population of the lions increased and now as we can see today, it had helped the beasts to save themselves from the extinction."

As we got deeper and deeper in the forest, the surroundings got more and more natural as if there was no existence of civilization. There was pin drop silence. The only noise was of the humming of the Jeep engine. Sometime we heard a bird chirping nearby or a cricket hidden in the tree. For me, it was like entering another world. The narrow path extending in front of the open Jeep flanked by trees and shrubs on either sides was so picturesque, that for the moment I felt simply content to be there; lions or no lions!

"If a jungle safari brings to your mind the vision of dense green foliage, then you would be surprised, for Gir is a dry deciduous and semi-arid forest with the majority of flora being teak wood trees. You will get to see a lot of dry thorny shrubs and dry grass, which is an excellent camouflage for the lions as well as the second largest predator in Gir, which is Leopard.

The other main carnivores in Gir include the Jungle Cat, Hyena, Jackal, Mongoose, Civet Cat and Ratel, which are quite difficult to spot. Amongst prey animals, you will come across a lot of Chital, Sambar Deer, and Monkeys, and if you go to the Kankai Temple, which is in the heart of the forest, you may get to see the shy Nilgai.

The resident avifauna species count in Gir is three hundred. Out of these, the most easily spotted species are the Yellow Footed Green Pigeon, the Rose Ringed Parakeet, the Ibis, the Indian Pitta, Tickell's Blue Flycatcher and the Black Rumped Flameback. Besides the Asiatic Lion, Gir also has the largest population of the once endangered Marsh Crocodile."

As we drove on, gradually, animals started appearing from behind the dry forests. Chitals, Sambhars, Langur monkeys, and many birds, but not the king himself – the lion. I was just beginning to believe that perhaps it was not my lucky day for the beast, when a tracker came and tipped our guide that he had spotted a lion!

"Gir forest is very rich in flora and fauna and houses about four hundred species of plants, thirty eight species of mammals, around three hundred species of birds, thirty seven species of reptiles and more than two thousand species of insects!" He continued.

"Population estimates of lion given before 1936 were only estimations based on personal knowledge. The first organized census conducted in 1936 showed a population of two hundred and eight seven lions. The onslaught of human pressure resulted into shrinkage of the Lion's habitat and now what remains with us is the Gir as the last refuge of the endangered mammal."

As we took in the surroundings we noticed that trees surrounding us which had been dense until now had all of a sudden disappeared leaving a vast open ground of dried grass few inches above a feet in height. It was then that our jeep suddenly stopped and our driver turned off the engine.

"Look in the Grass." Whispered the armed guard pointing towards the grass.

All the eyes in the jeep turned to the spot around three hundred meters from our jeep, which the guard was pointing. In the beginning, nothing appeared to me but as soon as my eyes got familiar with the view, I distinguished the figure of an animal, which had blended in with the surroundings. It was a lion.

I knew it was a lion because he had mane on it and from what I know about lions, lioness does not have the mane.

As soon as I saw him, I got my camera and started having the pics. I zoomed in to see the beast. His body was submerged in the grass. His legs were in the grass. His back was in opposite direction of ours, revealing a part of stomach towards us. He was gazing in his front, which revealed his side face to us, followed by his long mane. Neither his tail nor his back was visible.

"I think he is enjoying the meal he just had." Smit whispered.

"He hasn't had the meal." clarified the guide

"It is the position in which they generally relax. From what I see from here, he is young, may be two to three years at most!" he added.

"How do you know that?" Vimal asked him, surprised by the fact that he had assumed his age from this distance.

"It's his mane. The older the lion grows the longer gets its mane. These kings of the jungle can weigh between two hundred and fifty to five hundred and fifty pounds, depending on sex and age and can grow up to fourteen years old in the wild and over the age of twenty years old in captivity. They become capable of hunting at the age of two and, at their full growth, after five or six years.

Male lions are distinguishable for their impressive manes, which signifies their masculinity and reflects their health. The darker and thicker the mane, the healthier the lion. It allows the lions to appear stronger and frightening to warn off enemies, particularly humans. It is scientifically proven that lion with thick and dark mane gets to mate with more lionesses than the other one. Lions with no manes are either genetically inbred or have been castrated."

We stood there for a while taking in the scene, while the girls were giggling and blushing, still gossiping about the mating part. After few minutes, driver turned on the engine and we continued with the safari.

The flora kept on changing in the forest and along with the flora, fauna too changed. In the denser part of the forest, we saw more birds than that on grasses. We saw few Parakeets, Woodpeckers and few other bright colored birds whose names I did not know and never saw or heard of. Whereas on the grassy part of the forest which was not covered much with trees, we saw Peacock. On branch of tree skeleton, we saw an Eagle. We also saw group of Deer, Sambar, Antelopes and wild Boars grazing. We saw a Jackal too. However, we were not that lucky to see a Leopard. , During our ride, we also met some Maldharis, who lived in the forest. It was amazing that they only used a stick to protect themselves from wild animals.

"Why is the Asiatic Lion endangered?" Visha asked.

"As I had already said, Asiatic Lions once roamed free across Northern India, as far as Jharkhand in the east, up to Narmada River in the south and even in northern Morocco and Greece. However, these cats became an easy target of hunters owing to their sociable nature and their easily accessible habitat, and by the close of the last century; they were extinct in all of the other places, save Sasan Gir. The timely protection accorded by the Nawab of Junagadh in the early 1900s and earnest efforts by the Government of Gujarat in following years averted the extinction of this remarkable mammal species, so much so that today the park boasts of a healthy lion population of about four hundred, however, this species still faces threat from poachers."

At around 4:00 PM, when we were on the road back to main gate, a Lion, whose hair was even thicker and bigger than that of the first lion we had seen, blocked our path. It was the fourth lion we had seen that day. The first one was in grass, second we saw was retreating to forest. He disappeared so fast that I was not even able to capture his photo. The second one was in forest under a shade of a tree. He was yawning when we saw him and I had been lucky enough to capture his photos of yawning. He slowly retreated to nap as if he had nothing in the world to worry about.

Anyway, the fourth lion was the most majestic of all. He was walking on the dirt road just ahead of us. We slowed our Jeep and kept distance between the beast and us. We drove like that for few minutes until the beast stopped and sat there in the middle of the dirt road. We had no choice than to stop their too. When I asked the guide why we could not pass by, he said that it will hurt king's pride and will be offended, and there is nothing worse in the world than the offended beast. Hence, we had no option but to be there until the beast decide to get up and wander away in the forest.

"There are few stories related to the Lions that are famous. Let me tell you one of them while we are stuck here." Guide said.

"This takes place in Rome, where a Greek slave named Androcles, had escaped from his master and fled into the forest.

There he wandered for a long time until he was weary and completely spent with hunger and despair.

Just then, he heard a lion near him moaning, groaning, and at times roaring terribly.

Tired as he was, Androcles thought of leaving the place; but as he made his way through the bushes, he stumbled over the root of a tree and fell down lamed.

When he tried to get up, there he saw a lion coming towards him, limping on three feet and holding his forepaw in front of him.

Poor Androcles was in despair; he had no strength to rise and run away, and there was the lion coming upon him. But when the great beast came up to him, instead of attacking him, it kept on moaning and groaning and looking at Androcles, who saw that the lion was holding out his right paw, which was covered with blood and much swollen.

Looking more closely at it, Androcles saw a great big thorn pressed into the paw, which was the cause of all the lion's trouble.

Collecting all the courage he had, he seized hold of the thorn and drew it out of the lion's paw, who roared with pain when the thorn came out, but soon after found such relief from it that he fawned upon Androcles and showed, in every way that he knew, to whom he owed the relief.

Instead of eating him up, he brought him a young deer that he had slain, and Androcles managed to make a meal from it. For some time the lion continued to bring the game, he had killed to Androcles, who became quite fond of the huge beast.

However, one day, a number of soldiers came marching through the forest and found Androcles.

As he could not explain what he was doing, they took him prisoner and brought him back to the town from which he had fled. Here his master soon found him and brought him before the authorities.

Soon Androcles was condemned to death for fleeing from his master.

Now it used to be the custom to throw murderers and other criminals to the lions in a huge circus, so that the public could enjoy the spectacle of a combat between them and the wild beasts.

Hence, Androcles was also condemned to the lions, and on the appointed day, he was led into the Arena and left there alone with only a spear to protect him from the lion.

The Emperor was in the royal box that day and gave the signal for the lion to come out and attack Androcles.

However, when it came out of its cage and got near Androcles, what do you think it did?

Instead of jumping upon him, it fawned upon him and stroked him with its paw and made no attempt to do him any harm.

It was of course the lion, which Androcles had met in the forest.

The Emperor, surprised at seeing such a strange behavior in so cruel a beast, summoned Androcles to him and asked him how it happened that this particular lion had lost all its cruelty at his disposition.

Therefore, Androcles told the Emperor all that had happened to him and how the lion was showing its gratitude for his having relieved it of the thorn. Thereupon the Emperor pardoned Androcles and ordered his master to set him free, while the lion was taken back into the forest and let loose to enjoy liberty once more."

By the time the guide's story ended, the Lion started walking away towards the forest. I thought of how it would have felt to Androcleus when he had seen the lion walking towards him and then on realizing that this mighty animal was in pain and then helping him and be friend with him, until one-day, he returns to his prison, meet his end. I wondered how he had felt when the beast he thought was his end, was same friend he had saved once, and now saves him, and gives him a new beginning when everything was doomed

"Sometimes, it's amazing how kind these animals could be." Aastha said. "I think they are not as cruel as everyone say they are."

"Then you haven't seen the other side of them." Vimal said. "You have just heard of brighter side. The darker side remains hidden to you."

"Your friend is right." Guide said. "Everyone has a dark side. Human, god, animals, everyone. Now listen carefully to the story that shows their darker side." The guide said.

We sat there attentively, listening to the story while our Jeep drove through the forest.

"It is a traditional Zulu story of a boy named Jabu.

There was a young herd boy named Jabu. He took great pride in the way in which he cared for his father's cattle. His father had many cows - over twenty five to have a count!

It was quite a task to keep these silly creatures out of trouble, away from the farmer's corn and out of the dangerous roads. Jabu had some friends who also kept their fathers' cattle, but none of them had even half the herd Jabu did! And none of them were as careful as Jabu. It was a sign of Jabu's father's pride in his boy that he entrusted such a large herd to such a young boy.

One day as he sat atop a small hill watching the animals feed and braiding long thin strips of grass into bangles for his sisters, Jabu's friend Sipho came running to him.

'Have you heard the news, my friend?' panted Sipho.

Before Jabu could even answer, Sipho rushed on to tell him.

'Bhubesi, the lion, has been seen in these parts. Last night Bhubesi attacked and killed one of Thabo's father's cows. The men of the village are already setting traps for the beast!'

The news did not surprise Jabu. His keen eyes had seen the spoor of the lion -- his leftover kill, his prints here-and-there in the soft earth, his dung. Jabu had respect for the king of the beasts, and since Bhubesi's pattern was to hunt at night when the cattle was safely within the corral, Jabu had seen no reason to alert the village of Bhubesi's presence.

'I wonder,' thought Jabu to himself, 'what if the cow was not left out of the corral?'

Everyone knew that Thabo was a sloppy herd boy, a fellow who ran with his head in the clouds. He had many times before, left behind a cow or two when he took them for the graze.

'Come, friend!' Sipho urged, 'Come and put your cows away for the day and watch with me as the men set the traps!'

Jabu slowly shook his head as he looked at Sipho and smiled.

'You know me, friend,' he returned Sipho's address. 'I cannot put the cattle back into the corral so early in the day! They need to be driven to the river before they go home.'

Sipho smiled.

'Yes, I thought you would say this, but, I wanted to tell you anyway. I will see you later, friend, perhaps by the fire tonight!'

Then, Sipho ran toward the village with a final wave to Jabu.

Jabu began to gather the cows together. He waved his staff and gave a loud whistle. Each cow looked up, then after a moment's pause, slowly started to trudge toward Jabu. With a grin, Jabu began to take them to water.

Jabu bathed his feet in the cool refreshing river as the cows drank their fill. It was a fine sunny autumn day, and if his mind had not been so busy thinking about the lion and the traps the men were setting, Jabu would probably be shaping the soft river clay into small cow figurines for his young brother. Then Jabu heard a sound that stole his breath from him.

'Rrrrroar!' came the bellow.

The cows all froze, a wild look coming into their eyes.

'Rrrroarrrrrrr....'

It was Bhubesi, and he was near!

There was no time to drive the animal's home; the lion was much too close. Jabu slowly rose, looking carefully around, his hand clenched on his staff. He walked purposefully, trying not to show the fear that made his knees tremble, pulling the cattle together into a tight circle. The cows trusted him and they obeyed.

'Rrrrroar...oarr...oarr...aaa!'

Jabu listened. Bhubesi was not declaring his majesty or might; it sounded more like a cry for help. After few more bellows, Jabu knew, Bhubesi was in trouble. Somehow, this took most of the boy's fear from him. Gripping his staff, Jabu quietly began to walk toward the lion's cry.

Yes, indeed, the lion was in trouble. Jabu found him in a small clearing several meters across the river. He was in one of the traps laid by the men of the village. His head was firmly wedged in the barred structure, and the more he struggled, the tighter the snare became.

Jabu stood and stared. Never before had he seen the king of the animals so near. He truly was a majestic animal, and a large part of his heart was sore for the creature. Then the lion saw the boy.

'Oh! Boy! It is good that you are here. Please, help me. I am in this stupid trap and I cannot free myself. Please, please, will you come and pull up on the bar that is holding my head here. Please!'

Jabu looked into Bhubesi's eyes. He could not read them, but he could hear the desperation in the animal's voice.

'Please, Boy! Please! Before those hunters come and kill me. Please release me!'

Jabu had a tender heart, but he was no fool.

'I would very much like to free you, Bhubesi! But I am afraid that as soon as I did so you would make me your dinner.' Jabu said.

'Oh, no, my friend! I could never eat someone who set me free! I promise I really promise with full sincerity, that I will not touch a hair on your head!'

Well, the lion begged and pleaded so pitifully that Jabu finally decided to trust him and set him free. Gingerly he stepped over to the trap and raised the bar that held the lion's head. With a mighty bound, the lion leapt free of the trap and shook his mane.

'Oh, thank you, boy! I really owe you something. My neck was getting so stiff in there, and I fear, my body would have parted from my head by the hunters, if you had not come along. Now, please, if you do not mind, boy, one last thing.... I have become so thirsty from being in that thing; I would really like a drink of water. Can you show me where the river is? I seem to have become confused with my directions.'

Jabu agreed, keeping a wary eye on the lion, he led the lion upstream from where he had come, away from his father's cows, since Bhubesi had made no promise about not eating them!

As lion drank, he watched Jabu with one eye.

He was thinking to himself, 'Hmmm...! Nice looking legs on that boy! Hmmm...! Those arms are good looking too! Pity to waste such an excellent meal!'

When the lion raised his head from the river, his both eyes were on Jabu, and this time the boy could see what it reflected. Jabu began to back up.

'You promised, Bhubesi,' Jabu began. 'I saved you from the hunters, and you promised not to eat me!'

'Yes,' said Bhubesi, slowly walking toward the retreating boy. 'You are right, I did make that promise, but somehow, now that I am free it does not seem so important to keep that promise. I am awfully hungry!'

'You are making a big mistake,' said Jabu. 'Don't you know that if you break your promises that the pieces of the broken promises will come back to pierce you?'

The lion stopped and laughed. 'Hah! What nonsense! How can such a flimsy thing pierce me? I am more determined than ever to eat you

86

now, boy,' and he started stalking Jabu once more, 'and all this talk is just serving to make me hungrier!'

Just then, an old donkey happened to pass across their path.

'Ask the donkey,' said Jabu to the lion. 'Ask him and he will tell you how bad it is to break a promise.'

'All right, you! You are certainly dragging this thing out! So I will ask the donkey.'

The lion turned to the old creature.

'I want to eat this boy,' he addressed the donkey. 'Isn't that okay?'

Jabu broke in, 'But he promised to let me go after I freed him from the snare,' Jabu added.

The donkey slowly looked at the lion and then at Jabu.

'I say,' the donkey started, 'that all my life these stupid humans have beat me and forced me to carry things. Now that I am old they turn me out and leave me to waste away all alone. I do not like humans.'

He turned back to the lion.

'Eat the boy, I say!' and the donkey moved on.

'Well, it settles then,' said the lion as he began to approach the boy once more.

Just then Mpungushe, the jackal stepped between the two.

'Oh, terribly sorry,' he said, 'to have disturbed you. I'll be on my way...'

'No!' shouted Jabu. 'Wait and tell the lion how bad it is to break a promise.'

'A promise?' asked the jackal. 'Well, I suppose it depends upon the promise, doesn't it? Why? Did one of you make a promise?'

Lion sat down and rolled his eyes up toward the heavens.

'Yes,' Jabu said, and he told Jackal how he had freed the lion from the trap, and how Lion had promised not to eat him, and how now Lion was intent upon doing that very thing!

'Oh, what a silly story!' said Jackal. 'Bhubesi, the great king of all the animals, stuck in a little trap made by humans? Impossible! I don't believe it.'

'It is true,' said Bhubesi. 'It is a strong and terrible trap!'

'Oh, I can't believe anything is stronger than my king. I must see this thing! Please, will you take the courtesy before your dinner to show me the trap of which you speak? Please! Then you can eat your meal in peace!'

Therefore, the lion, keeping Jabu in front of himself, led Jackal to the trap.

'You can't tell me that this little thing could actually hold your head! Never! I just cannot imagine it. My king, would you mind just sticking your head there so I can see how you looked when the boy found you?'

'You are taxing me with your questions. This last thing I will do for you and then you must be on your way and leave me to my dinner in peace.'

Therefore, Lion stuck his head back between the bars just the way he had been when Jabu had found him. Then, quicker than lightning, Jackal threw the top bar in place. Lion was in a trap, once again!

'Yes,' said Jackal, 'now I see how you were trapped, and what a pity, that you are trapped once again. However, the boy is right, Bhubesi. Broken promises always catch up with you!'

Lion roared in anger, but the sound trap held him well. Jabu thanked the jackal and ran back to his cows, who were all patiently waiting for their shepherd's return.

Jabu drove them home and into the corral. What a day he had!

'Jabu, Jabu,'

Sipho came running from behind Jabu.

'The lion has been caught in the trap near the river! You and your cows missed all the adventure!'

Jabu turned and smiled at his friend.

'We had all the adventure we need for one day,' he said.

Sipho headed back to the hunters to hear the story once again of the mighty lion caught in the trap, while Jabu greeted his mother in the cooking house and sat down with a sigh."

We were all lost in the story. The Lion Bhubesi, boy Jabu, Jackal, it was a very scary story to make anyone fear an animal.

"Now what do you think of the Bhubesi?" Guide continued. "Would you dare to help him? Would Androcles have helped the lion if he had heard of this story?"

We sat there in silence taking in all that the guide had just said.

"I don't know." I finally said. "Maybe Androcleus would have helped the lion or maybe he wouldn't have."

"Exactly." The Guide said. "We cannot predict animals as we cannot predict all humans. We just need to think about ourselves. In both the stories, animals got help, but one saved his savior and other tried to kill the savior. However, what both stories tell in common is that either you will have to pay for your actions or will be rewarded for.

In first story, Androcleus earned a life by saving one. Whereas in other story, Bhubesi had to pay for betraying. The only thing we need to know is our actions makes our future."

Five minutes later, our vehicle came across another three lionesses and two cubs walking on the track ahead. It was indeed like witnessing royalty, and just like one would be tongue tied in front of kings and queens, I felt totally at a loss of words in front of the regal beast. One of the lionesses sat down on the track to the left of our vehicle like a sentinel; unmoved by all the gawking and subdued oohs and aahs that were emitting around her. After allowing us to have her pics, she coolly walked away following the rest of the pride into the bushes.

At the end of the day's safari, we were lucky enough to have a glimpse of the pride consisting of the three lionesses and two cubs twice on the same route, and four other lions, one walking and one sleeping. The lion with his marvelous mane remained elusive, giving only brief glimpses, and one more sleeping far away under a grove of trees. We had more luck with the leopards; spotting both a female and a male.

The other flora and fauna that we came across in the Gir National Park consisted of Sambar Deer, Nilgai, Marsh Crocodile, Gum trees, Saledi trees, Banyan trees, Termite hills, Rose-Ring Parakeets, Yellow Footed Green Pigeons, the Ibis, the Lapwing and many more birds the names of which are unknown to me.

Soon, our first day of the safari ended. Out of thirty-six species of mammals, three hundred species of birds and thirty-seven species of reptiles in the forest, we had hardly seen one-fifth of total species of fauna in the forest. However, we were the luckiest tourist ever to spot so many lions in a day. Jigar's Jeep had hardly a luck of witnessing two lioness and no Lions.

After dropping off the guide at the park gate, our jeep drove us to our resort. We took our dinner and sat out at campfire listening to songs. When we were tired enough, we all left for our room for the night bidding goodnight to each other. We had enough for the day and it was time for a peaceful sleep.

\*

Later in the room, I woke up suddenly from my sleep when Smit and Vimal were talking about something.

Few minutes later, they both went to sleep. I closed my eyes and tried to remember what had woke me up. However, I could not remember anything. I again closed my eyes and tried to sleep. Soon I was asleep and different shapes and pictures started taking shape in my mind.

In my dream, I was at the entrance gate and it appeared as if that was a reality and nothing had ever happened in the morning. It appeared as if that day did not exist at all.

Everything was same as it had been in the morning.

We passed the entrance gate and joined the queue.

I saw the cage and in it the beast that was sleeping in the corner.

I took out my camera and started capturing the pics.

Suddenly I remembered what had happened in the morning. It was that moment when the kid had thrown the toy. I realized it and

91

turned to stop the kid but he already had thrown the toy towards the beast.

Time slowed as the toy glided through the air towards the king.

It moved down.

It stuck the king.

The beast opened his eyes that was full of anger.

He got up and started charging towards me instead of the kid.

As time went on slowly, his form got bigger and bigger until he collided his massive body with the cage bar. With the clang, time switched to its normal pace.

Everything was happening as it had in the morning. Except for the fact that the lion had its eyes focused on me.

Guard saw the incident and went in the post to bring out the gun.

The king was getting up for the second round. It was time for the shot from the gun that never came, and the beast banged the bars more furiously.

Everything changed from then.

I turned my head towards the guard.

The guard who was supposed to fire the shot was kneeling down to pick the gun that I do not know how but was on the ground.

I turned my gaze towards the bars, which already had loosened its grip due to two previous collisions.

The beast banged the bars with all his might this time and with the deafening sound, the bars gave up the grip.

It came off leaving open field for the king.

He charged towards the kid.

Oh no, it was not the kid.

He had his gaze fixed on me.

He charged towards me.

My legs were transfixed in its position and I was unable to move myself.

With a roar, the king leaped in the air towards me.

Time slowed as did everything else.

Everything slowed in front of me.

I saw the guard who had picked his gun aimed at the beast.

The kid was on verge of tears from his eyes, filled with the fear.

Seeing the king in the air with shock and fear, Smit, Aastha, Vimal, Shivani, Visha and everyone else were perplexed on their place. Every eyes in the park was on the king.

I saw it too, but I was the only one who was closest to him, who saw the anger in his eyes, who was facing the sharp bloodthirsty teeth.

As time passed he moved closer to me slowly but steadily.

Every head too moved slowly.

I tried to move away faster but failed.

Maybe my mind had freed itself from the bond of time, but my body was still in coordination with time that moved slowly.

At last, his paws stuck me and I was up in the air and out of the jeep with the king.

As I was up in the air, I closed my eyes, which was not ready for anything more fearful.

I landed on the dirt road slowly that bought tremendous pain in my back and heard few of my bones crack.

I opened my mouth to let my pain escape through my mouth but before a sound could escape my throat, I felt a sharp pain on my neck as hot blood burst out through the opening madewith the piercing of the beast's teeth.

He had covered my neck with his half-open jaw.

I heard two shots from the gun, which was actually too late in timing.

I opened my eyes for last time and saw beautiful mane of the beast in front of my eyes, which appeared golden with the sun light.

With that last beautiful sight of the golden mane, I closed my eyes, which were to remain shut, forever.

My pain, my panic, and my fear, everything left my body along withmy soul.

I woke with a startle.

Although we were sleeping with air conditioner at its full and ceiling fan at its max, I was soaked up in perspiration. At first, everything was dark in front of me, as if I really had died. I bought my hand to check my heart, which was beating rapidly.

I let my eyes adjust to the darkness. As it got adjusted to the darkness with the light that came from the moon that was three nights away from full moon, I could make out things in the room. I saw table, I saw mirror, I saw cupboard in the corner, and I saw everything else that was in the room. On the couch, Vimal was snoring peacefully. Next to me, Smit and Brijesh were fast asleep.

I picked up the water bottle next to my bed and went out in the gallery.

I felt the cool breeze and waited for my heart to calm. I drank few gulps of water and watched the beautiful moon in the clear sky. I focused on the stars next to it to occupy my mind.

After few minutes when my heart was beating normally, I went back to the room and retired to my bed. I closed my eyes and let my thoughts roam free. I waited for the nightmare to come back, but instead only darkness came and with that darkness, I finally drifted away into emptiness.

*

## CHAPTER 7

I felt the cool breeze on my face as our Jeep drove for the National park. We had all occupied our respective Jeeps. At the park gate, we completed the procedure for clearance and were soon on our way to the forest. Today along with a guide, and the guard, another armed man joined in, who directly took his place at the front. He paid attention to no one and no one paid attention to him. It was as if he did not existed. As we entered through the forest, flora kept on changing in same way as it had on the day before. There was strange silence in atmosphere. It was not peaceful as it had the day before. Maybe it was just my imagination or was a result of the silence in our Jeep. No one was speaking anything.

As we passed, we saw few Deer and group of Sambal, grazing. Today we were lucky to have glimpse of a Leopard. The guard had spotted it when he was retreating into the forest. He pointed his finger at him and as I followed his finger, I was able to capture one photo of the cat as it disappeared in the forest. Later I showed that photo to Smit and Vimal, who praised the moment that I had snapped in my camera.

Further, into the forest, we started climbing up the low hills. On the way up, we came to a river stream. This was not the first source of water in the forest that we had seen in the park. We had seen few of the check dams in the forest earlier. The stream was not deep. We can clearly see the bottom of the stream and fish swimming in it. It was hardly deep until my waist. As it flowed through the forest, it generated soft music of the water. I enjoyed the sound of water rippling through the trees.

We were driving on the dirt path of the hill against the flow of water. Soon the cliff we were driving on got steeper and steeper and after driving on the road for few more minutes, we had reached the top of the hill. The stream was few feet below and had taken a shape of mini-river. Again, in few meters, the mini-river had disappeared and had taken up the shape of a small river. What we had seen earlier must have been a minor tributary of this one.

I saw small herd of deer drinking water from the river. I focused my camera on them but as I zoomed in, I noticed a movement on the other end of the shore. I searched for the source and soon located it. One big marsh crocodile had come out of the bushes around the bank and silently disappeared into water. I asked the driver to stop the Jeep, so that we can see the events that was about to unravel before us.

I focused my eyes on water but failed to see anything. I switched to the camera and focused on water. I zoomed in and searched for few seconds. The water was still except for ripples from deer's side. It appeared as if there was no one there, except for the herd of deer. There was no sign of crocodile. However, all of sudden there were new ripples in the water. Minor one yet I saw them. Then I saw pair of eyes floating in the water. No it was not only one pair, there were two. One of it was coming from the direction where I had seen the crocodile disappear. Another was coming from its right side.

I moved my camera in the direction in which they were headed which were obviously, where the herd was drinking.

They were moving towards the herd without making any noise or showing any hint of their presence. They quickly covered the distance. On the other hand, the herd of deer was drinking water peacefully unaware of the upcoming threat.

All of a sudden, their peacefulness was shattered when a crocodile emerged out of water and grabbed a leg of one of the deer. At same time, other one too emerged from other side and grabbed the leg of other deer. Frightened of the sudden outburst, other members of the herd, who were still free, ran away and disappeared in the forest. However, one of the calf had stopped on its way. It turned back to the crocodiles expecting if the other deer will escape somehow from the jaws of their predator. To his disappointment, both of the victims lay dead in the jaws of the crocodiles. It belled out at bodies as if calling them to get up but the bodies gave no response to his call. The way it looked at the dead ones reminded me of how I had looked at my parent's photos after cremating their bodies, hoping that it all will turn out to be just a horrible nightmare and next morning will find them next to me when I open my eyes. They must have been its parents or something because I can surely somehow, see pain in its eyes as it turned and disappeared behind the trees.

I felt pity for the kid. Our condition was same. It too was now orphaned in same way I had been few years ago. I wondered if it would feel the pain that I had felt when my parents died. I wondered if it would feel the loneliness that I had felt. I wondered if it would have nightmares, the way I get at night. I wondered if it felt the way I did when I had just discovered that my parents had died. I wondered if it would have any feelings in few days or just forget about his parents in process of saving itself from some other predator. I wondered if he would be able to survive without his parents for rest of his life, or for few years, or even few days, before another carnivore had hunted him down. Whatever the future holds for the kid, there was nothing anyone can do. It was the rule of life. Stronger one takes down the weaker one, let it be richer and poor or carnivore and herbivore.

We continued with the safari. Everyone sat in silence as earlier. Everyone was lost in his or her own world. The driver had focused his eyes on the roads and the guard in front was keeping an eye around to locate any possible danger.

We drove past the trees alongside the river, which had now turned from a minor one to a major one with width of few meters and depth enough to drown a dinosaur.

After ride of few minutes, we came to a dam. The reservoir was full with water. As we drove, we saw that it had many outlet points, but the main and the biggest was the one from which we had come. We drove through main outlet, which was a total curve towards a building that lay few kilometers ahead of us. While driving we saw that the reservoir had many other outlets along with the main outlet. These outlets provided water to small streams, which further ran through the forest.

"It's Kamleshwar Dam.," said the guide.

"It is the main source of water for the park. These Dam provides water to many streams and rivers in the forest. It is home for crocodiles and their population is numerous in the depths."

I stared in the water for any sign of crocodile in the dam but there was none. I imagined thousands of crocodile resting at the depths of the dam. The very thought scared me. I shifted from my seat and sat as far away as possible from the water. They must be somewhere in the water, or in the woods nearby the reservoir, or in the streams that flows from the reservoir.

We travelled on the concrete structure of the dam. It was huge. After travelling a circle of few hundred meters around the dam, we came to the checkpoint. We stopped there.

Checkpoint was an old building that was constructed on the edge near the forest. Somewhere nearby, there must be a water outlet point because I heard the sound of the water bursting out from the hole.

"It's break time." Guide said. "You'll get drinks and snacks in there. Just don't throw the wrappers in the forest."

He and the guard left us and went to the checkpoint. There was only one empty Jeep parked outside of the checkpoint.

"Come on. Let's go, let's get some snacks!" Smit said.

"I'm not hungry!" I said. "You all take break. I'll take a look around."

"You sure?" Vimal asked.

"Yeah!" I replied.

They all left except for the Shivani.

"What's the matter?" She asked.

"I don't know." I said.

"What's it?" She asked again.

"I don't know." I said again. "I feel like I am missing something. I have no idea of what it is. I just feel like there is something amiss with me. Maybe it's nothing or maybe it's just in my mind, but it does not feel right or maybe it's something about the hunt that we had seen at the stream earlier."

"Don't think about it." She said. "Just stay with me and everything will be alright."

She kissed me on the head, and held my hands in hers.

"You want anything?" she asked.

"No. I will be fine. You be with others and I will join you in a moment."

She nodded and left for the checkpoint.

I took my camera and started taking the pics of the surroundings to clear my head. The dam provided a great view. Behind the dam, there were hills covered with the trees and the dam itself was too beautiful.

Once I was done with, the reservoir and the hills beyond, I turned my camera to the trees nearby. Since the previous day, I was trying to get a close view of wilderness and today I got the chance to capture it in my camera. I took close up from in between the trees. Then I turned to trees and then to the sky from the gaps between the trees.

After that, I searched for the water outlet. I walked in the direction of the sound and soon few meters from the jeep, reached at the point. The water was bursting out with tremendous pressure. The water flowed through the hills and disappeared behind the trees with a curve few meters ahead. I took the photos of the curve and the stream first, and then turned to the mouth of the outlet. Obviously, nothing was visible but still, I took few pictures of it. Soon my lens got wet with water droplets.

I took out my handkerchief from the pocket to rinse off the droplets. Before I could complete rinsing off water from the lens, I dropped my camera on the ground when all of a sudden a hand covered my mouth and held me tightly through my neck.

"Stay quiet or you will lose your life." came the voice from behind me.

The voice of the stranger asked me to calm down and turned me around as I struggled to help myself on my feet.

It was the man with the gun. He had a knife around my neck.

"Stay as it is or you'll feel how smoothly it cuts." He said and again turned me around.

I stood there, struggling my way to get out of his grip. I was unable to shout at all. If I somehow manage to free myself from him, and shout out for help, chances of help coming was as low as nil. I calculated safe passages for me to get me out of this situation. I thought of kicking him, and then screaming out for help, but I realized that it would be too late before anyone could come to my rescue. Even if someone might, the man had a knife and a gun to overpower anyone. Hence, there was no hope of rescue for me and I was on my own.

I had no fear of facing the death because I myself had tried to end my life so many times in the past. So next thing I decided to do was what tough female actors pretend to do in movies to run away in situation like this. I pulled my waist forward and pushed it with full force against the man. The man lost his balance and retreated few steps. Taking the advantage of the situation I hit him in the face with one hand and with second hand gave a hard blow on his wrist.

As a result, he dropped the weapon that he held in his hand. He came forward with a punch, which I managed to dodge, sending him behind me with a back kick. The momentum bought me near the weapon. I kneeled down and picked it up. I turned back holding the weapon in my hand. I turned to the guide who had already held up his hands. It was now my turn to control the situation.

I pointed the knife at him.

"You don't have a stand against me." He said with a crooked smile.

"Ah. I won't be so sure." I said and tried to attack him with the knife.

I tried to jab him with full force but he was too fast for me. Before I could even touch him, he had already moved from his place and held my wrist in his hand. Then he turned my wrist towards sky giving me too much pain to bear. I tried to punch him, but before I could do anything, he slapped me on my face. He pulled me up and threw me in the air with all of its strength and next thing I knew after that was, I was floating in the air and then moving down towards the water that was thrusting out from the hole.

*

# CHAPTER 8

Never in my life had I imagined that I would have to face such a circumstances. I had so many times thought of ending up my life but had never thought of the way, and the way that I was facing right now was not the one that I prefer.

As soon as I was in the thrusting water, it dragged me away with its flow. I went directly into the water and after few moments when I came out, I had already moved far away from the concrete wall of the dam. There was no sign of the gunman because of whom I was in this situation. Before I could regain my strength, I had passed the curve and the concrete wall had disappeared behind trees. I turned from that direction and when I saw what lay ahead of me, a chill of panic ran down my spine. Few yards ahead, lay a waterfall and I would not be surprised if I do not make it through. I was already feeling tired of keeping myself floating so I made no effort of swimming. Instead, I just closed my eyes and waited for the inevitable to take place.

For few moments, I felt nothing as I fell from the waterfall. After that, I hit the water, which felt like concrete floor. After that, next thing that I remember was lying on the riverbank completely spent. I had no idea of how, I had managed to swim all the way to the bank, but somehow I had made it and I was not going to drown. I was sure that I was safe here because crocodiles will not live too near to falls and no other animal would come here to drink water. They will prefer slow and smooth waters. Therefore, I closed my eyes and let my body relax.

I had no idea when I fell asleep but when I opened my eyes again, it was already getting dark. By that time, my clothes had dried up and sand had covered them. I sat up, washed my hands, face, and cleansed my clothes of sand. I felt thirsty so I quenched my thirst and filled my stomach with water. Then I picked up the knife that somehow I had bought all the way along with me. I searched if I had anything else with me, to which, I only found the thread on my wrist that Panditji had tied. Other than that, everything was either in water or at the dam wall.

"You'll face a hard time…" Panditji had said.

Maybe he knew this is going to happen or maybe he had bribed the gunman for this. Maybe he had nothing to do with it, and it was only the gunman or maybe this was all part of the journey that he was talking in the first place. Whatever it may be, right now, I had to get out of this mess and make my way out of the forest. After that, I will see of what to do with Panditji for this.

I scanned for any escape route.

I found none.

I looked at my surrounding. I saw the waterfall and any possible path to get away from wherever I was. I thought of climbing up the waterfall and getting back to the checkpoint. I could take help of the guards there and get out of the forest.

I placed the knife between my teeth to free both of my hands. I started climbing up the waterfall, holding whatever I found strong enough to hold the grip and not too slippery to slip off.

I was halfway there when I saw a figure at the top of the waterfall. A man stood there giving out his hand to help me. I was so happy to see someone at my rescue, but when I saw the face of the helping hand, fear took over my senses.

It was the man with the gun. He had a big smirk of victory on his face.

"Let me help you." He said.

His voice made me lose my grip. I fell on the ground. Every part of my body was in pain.

I looked up again and saw him pointing his gun at me. Despite of all the pain, I stood up and ran as fast as I could. Tears rolled down my eyes. Thought of running into a Leopard or Monkey or Lion or any other animal never occurred in my mind. Only thought that occurred to me and only thing I wanted was to get rid of this person, and get back to my friends.

When I finally stopped running, it was already dark. I wanted to go on but I cannot walk in the forest all on my own in the night. It was sign for me to find some place for shelter, and there is no place safe in the forest. So instead, I must find some place, which is less dangerous to camp out. It was not that I was afraid of dying, or maybe I was, but I knew that if I wanted to die, I wanted it to be in peace, not like this or any other manner that I had seen in my nightmares.

Anyway, now that I had decided to take shelter in the forest, I prepared myself for the night. I brought some long leaves and made a bed out of it on a tree branch. Then I closed my eyes and waited for sleep to come. However, it never came. Maybe because I already had enough rest, or the feeling that I was sleeping on a tree on the bed of leaves all on my own in a forest full of carnivores, was keeping me awake. Whatever the reason, I kept my eyes close and let my thoughts take over my mind.

At times, I sat upright on hearing a sound nearby, but on seeing nothing around and deciding that it was nothing but the wind; I relaxed back on my bed. Once, for a moment, I thought that I saw two glowing eyes staring at me but next moment it was gone. It might have been anything or might have been nothing or it might have been an illusion, but whatever that thing was, it never appeared again. Again, I went to my fruitless effort of sleep.

Everything was so silent and still that it felt as if I was sleeping in a movie set of some horror scene in jungle. I closed my eyes in silence for few moments and then heard a deafening roar.

I was just having the peaceful moments of my day and this roar ruined it all. I fell off from the tree branch onto the ground.

Again the deafening roar came.

The moment I heard it, I started running.

Again, another roar.

This time, it was clearer and coming from somewhere nearby. Instead of running away from the death, I had run into the death. I thought in my mind that if the thread was supposed to protect me, it was failing at the task very seriously. I kept on walking, trying to avoid the source of the roar. But out of my luck, I directly ran into the beast who was making it.

In front of me, their lay the beast. His right rear paw, trapped in some kind of toothed iron clamp. I was glad that there was that clamp holding the lion in its grip. The lion might have killed me in my sleep, if not for this clamp, or, he might have just wondered away. I tried to think of the positive thingsthat could have happened but failed at the task. How was I supposed to thinkof the good outcome in situations, if the bad one was the obvious one? Whatever that could have happened, the fate right now was with me.

I stood there as a statue. I had no idea of what to do. I remembered the stories that the guide had told us on the first day of the safari.

Another roar came from the lion, which clearly yelled the pain he was suffering from. He had seen me and was staring at me. Pain clearly showed in his eyes. My heart felt pity for him. However, my logic shouted in my mind to run away. It was same for me right now, as it had been for Androcleus and Jabu, but the problem was that I had no idea of the outcome that my decision might make. Would it be like that of Androcleus with a happy conclusion or that of Jabu with end of my life? I closed my mind and thought of what to do next.

I listened as my heart and my logic argued with each other. On one side, my mind was asking me to run away and not to be as stupid as Jabu. Things that happened to Androcleus, happens only in fairy tales. On the other hand, my heart asked me to help him and show some humanity. After all, humanity made humans different from the animals. If not, there would be no difference in humans and animals. It was confusing me of what to do next.

I opened my eyes and saw directly into the eyes of the beast. For a moment I thought, that, the beast had been crying all along until my arrival and its eyelids were still wet. However, that must have been my imagination because I had never heard of a crying lion. Anyway, when I looked into its eyes and saw its pained expression, I finally made my mind that I need to help him whatever may be the outcome; I had to help the beast. This was the time to check whether the thread on my wrist was doing its work or not.

Therefore, against all the logical reasoning of my mind to run away, I walked towards the lion. I took my every step cautiously and looked directly into its eyes. I had once read that by looking directly into the eyes of animals, you could easily win their trust. I raised my both hand to show him that I did not want to hurt him.

He tried to stand up and gave an angry growl at me.

I wondered what was wrong with him. I was trying to him and he was growling at me, but, then I realized of his fear, when I realized of the knife that I held in my mind.

"No, I am here to help." I said and threw the knife on the ground.

"Don't kill me and I'll free you from your misery."

I had no idea why I was talking to him. He was not going to understand me. He was just an animal, a dumb animal who kills, but whatever the reason maybe, I talked to him. May be it was to confide myself that I could do this and survive it.

"If you promise me that you won't hurt me I will free you." I spoke again.

I stared at him for response but nothing came. Instead, he kept on staring at me, which was clear that he had not understood anything.

At last considering his blank stare as his response, I carefully got close to him, and tried to open the clamp with my hands.

I failed.

It was much tougher than I had thought. I tried repeatedly, and repeatedly I failed. This was not working. The grip was too strong for me and the clamps hurt my finger.

I looked around and picked up the knife. The lion growled with fear.

"I'm not hurting you," I said, "I am trying to help."

He calmed down and I tried to open the clamps with the knife between the tooth clamps.

I failed, again.

I again inserted it at the end. With all my might, I pulled the driver up. Slowly as my face got red, the clamp too opened slightly. Finally, when it was enough for the beast to pull his leg out, he took his paws out of the clamp. I pulled out the knife and the clamp closed down all empty.

I was relieved. After all this efforts, I had finally freed him.

On getting rid from the clamp, the king tried to get up on its feet, but lost the balance and fell down again. I tried to help him but backed away immediately when I got a blank stare from him. I was still sitting near the clamp. He turned towards me and saw directly into my eyes.

For a moment, we held each other's gaze. I thought I had made a mistake and he is going to consume me for his dinner. Instead, he turned and tried again. This time, somehow, he managed to get up on three legs. He was so majestic and beautiful. He was the biggest lion that I had ever seen. The lions that I had seen during the safari were nothing compared to him. His mane was shining in the moon light, and he was trying to stand still. Somehow, he regained his strength and I watched him with awe, as it limped towards the trees. He stood there and turned at me. After taking one last glance in my direction, he limped away in silence and disappeared behind the trees.

During all that time, I sat there next to the clamp. I wondered who would have planted such deadly clamps in the forest. It was dripping with the lion's blood. I took a deep breath and glanced away from it. I got up and started walking in an unknown direction. It was still dark and I cannot roam in the forest at night. Therefore, I climbed on one of the neem tree. It would be safest place for me to stay alive if any animal passes from here. Lions and any other carnivores cannot climb on the tree except for leopard, and of monkeys, I do not fear them when I have much more dangerous animals to worry.

I sat on the branch and looked up at the sky through the leaves. Stars were shining brightly. It was going to be very tough night for me. I felt the cool breeze against my skin and thought about the night that lay in front of me. Finally, I closed my eyes wondering when the night will end. The main question that rose now was, will I be alive to see the rising sun, or would be dead by then.

I had helped a beast and saved his life. I wondered if the beast would help me, if the need might come. I had no answers to the questions that rose in my mind. I had hundreds of thoughts of my friends and my love. I wondered if they were out there searching for me or were they back to the resort. I wondered what the man with the gun had told them about my disappearance. All this thoughts filled my mind.

For whole night, I tried to get some sleep closing my eyes but my every effort was in vain. In the end, I ended up staring at the trees half of the time. For other half time, I let my thoughts loose until my thoughts broke down with hustling of leaves or from a cry of an animal somewhere in the forest. Whenever I heard a sound, I tightened my grip around the knife, my only weapon, to fight against anything that might come from anywhere, but thank god, that, I never had to use my weapon. With every moment that passed with the night, I got more and more frightened. I wondered when something would appear from somewhere and bring death to me, but that never happened and I remained alive. Soon, I saw first rays of sunlight from the trees and with it, balloons of joy busted out in my heart. At last, the darkness had vanished and sun had brought new rays of hope along with it.

Never had I felt so happy to see sun shine in the sky like that. However, today it felt so nice, just to see sun shine in the sky. The sun was same and doing same thing that it had done since eons, but today, it felt as if it had shone up especially for me and now I could easily make out the surroundings. It amazed me how much difference it could make to look at things from different angles. For many times in my life I had seen sun shine in sky but I had never felt like this, and just spending a night in darkness in woods made me realize the importance of sun. I wondered if someone somewhere might be thinking same things as I was thinking right now.

Once sun had completely rose, I got up, got fresh, and washed my face in the nearby stream. It was now time to head towards the gates. I looked at the stream, thought of going back to the waterfall, and try my luck with climbing over it all the way to checkpoint and check if guards can help me. However, in the end I decided against it because I knew that my luck always worked against me. Having made the decision, I started walking along the bank, to whatever place it might take me.

While walking I searched for any path or road or any sign of the vehicle that might have passed moments ago, but there was no sign or trace of human or vehicles. I sometimes heard something move nearby me in the trees but soon realized that it was just wind. It was then that I saw a moment in the bushes few meters from me. It appeared as if the bushes were dancing. I stopped and waited and moments later, it came again. This time it was louder and I felt it. There was some kind of low frequency vibrations, which was vibrating the ground as well as water. It appeared as if water was dancing in front of my eyes. I felt the vibrations as it came and soon everything returned to normal.

I stood there for another wave of vibrations to come but it never came. Instead, there came the animal that I did not want to see. Few meters from me, a marsh crocodile emerged out of nowhere and disappeared into the water without taking a single glance at me. It had not seen me so I was safe but feeling of seeing the reptile from so near without any boundaries in-between, was more than enough for me. I stood there stunned and shocked. A crocodile had just crossed my path, which was too much for me to believe.

I continued walking but kept safe distance between the water and me. I do not want to take chance with crocs. They might come out anytime from water or trees. However, I knew that they are more powerful in water than on land, so I have to keep as much distance from water as possible.

After few more yards, I heard the noise once again. This time it was not far from me. It came from bushes few meters behind me. Then suddenly a crocodile emerged from it. This time, it had seen me and seeing a meal ready to consume, it ran for me. I had realized what was about to happen and sprinted forward. I was too fast for the crocodile and missed those powerful jaws for inches. I ran and soon was out of his reach.

I turned and saw him chasing after me. I kept on running I saw few meters ahead, two crocodiles lying steady on the bank and having sunbath. I turned and saw that the crocodile was closing on me. In between, the crocodiles taking sunbath, and crocodile chasing me, I stood trapped.

I had no hope of escape. Ahead on my path, lay two most dangerous animals, behind my back, came another closing on after me, how far worse could this situation get. However, my bad situation got worse when all of a sudden, I heard a roar, and following the roar came a beast. It emerged out of the trees and started attacking the crocodile that was following me. It went directly for the crocodile's back. Seeing a surprise attack on itself, the crocodile counter attacked the beast with its powerful jaws, but the beast dodged it and so the fight between them began. Beast with his claws and croc with his jaws.

All that was happening around me was too much for me to process. Whichever of the animal is going to survive this fight, its next target will be me. As this two carnivore's were not enough, the crocodiles that were enjoying sunbath had their attention on the fight and me now. The roar had caught their attention and they had either decided to join the fight for their species or come and get meal out of me. They were either making their way towards the battlefield or making their way towards their meal. Whatever it was, I mas dead if I stood there.

Considering it as an only chance of escape, I sprinted into the forest. I had never thought I could run this fast but today my legs carried me as fast as it could from the faces of the death.

I ran continuously without turning back or paying attention to anything around me. I might have bumped into an animal but with mercy of god or the mercy of the thread on my wrist that Panditji had told, would protect me, I did not. Finally, once I was convinced that I was far from the danger, I stopped. I was breathing and sweating heavily. The forest, which had appeared beautiful to me the day before, now appeared much more dangerous than beautiful. On every step, there was something new and adventurous but if your luck is against you than you will find death awaiting you on every turn.

Once my breathing returned to normal, I continued walking into the forest. I did not know where I was going but kept on moving with hope that I will end up at human world, or at least on the path that will lead me to the one.

*

# CHAPTER 9

There was chirping of birds and rustling of leaves. I stood on the branch and looked around. I was starving and so had climbed on a mango tree to have something to eat. After eating three mangoes, I was searching for a source of water to satiate my thirst. There was none. I climbed higher and saw through the trees. Few meters away I saw a gap between the trees. I assumed it must be a river, a stream, or a path to civilization.

I climbed down the tree and started walking in the direction of the source. Holding the knife in one hand, I walked cautiously listening and searching for any sound of threat.

On the way, I saw monkeys jumping from one tree to another. There was a nightingale singing somewhere nearby. I saw few other species of bird, which I did not recognize. On one of the trees there was a woodpecker pecking the trunk. I was amazed of seeing so many things yet my mind had it focus on the path.

I thought of Shivani and my friends. I thought of how much fun we had. I remembered all the pleasant memories that we had made together. I thought of our time together in theaters, at college, at

115

parties. I thought of how foolish we were when we sat together. The foolish things we talked about, the girls we had crush on, professors that we hated, riding bicycles alongside the canal, late night studies during the exams, festivals that we had enjoyed together, bunking the college classes, all those things that made my life incredible. I smiled as I remembered those days of joy and fun. However, I have to focus on the present now. I could relive everything again if I get back out to the human world, and to do that, I have to focus.

After half an hour of walk, I came out of the dense forest. It was a stream with clear water. I walked to it and searched for any sign of crocodiles. On seeing none, I walked to the stream and quenched my thirst. Once my thirst was satiated, I washed my face. I sat there and saw fish swimming in the water. My thoughts still roamed around our days in college. After few moments, I stood up to leave still thinking about those days.

I was so engrossed with my thoughts that I had not noticed a lion emerging out of the trees. By the time I had noticed him, it was drinking water from the stream. That means it had not seen me either. My mind was not sure of what to do now. In one corner of my mind, I was still going through the beautiful moments of our college life and my other part was screaming out with fear. I wanted to smile as well as cry but was not sure of what to do. I knew that when the lion had filled himself, he would turn around and notice me. What I was not sure was what his reaction would be. I was not sure whether it would turn away and disappear behind the trees or will it run after me until it kills me down.

I prayed to god to make lion do the first because if it decided the second, it will surely overrun me. I could do nothing about that but accept what comes, and unable to decide what to do, I stood there paralyzed.

Once the beast had satiated his thirst, it turned to leave. While turning he saw me and paused. For a moment, he stood there and fixed his gaze on me. His gaze made me tremble with fear. I do not know why but I felt pure hatred in his gaze. Sensing my fear, it ran for me. With full sprint and might, it charged.

I stood there as the beast came closer and its form got larger. It was same as it had been on the day of beginning of safari. Except the beast in front of me was much more majestic than that in the cage and then that I had saved, and there were no bars between the beast and me. I held my knife in my hand, ready to use whenever I had chance.

Once he was close, he leaped in the air. With his jump, I felt time slowing as death neared me. He tilted his head on right and opened his mouth pointing for my neck. At same time, all of its nails came out of the paws.

His face was in front of me.

His claws inches from my chest.

His body in the air.

Seeing the death in front of me, I felt time slowing down again. I saw his face and jaws closing on me. As his paws made contact with my body, I lost my balance. His claws were starting to penetrate through my skin, but before it can penetrate any more, his face blurred and I saw an orange colored shadow in front of me and then with the same speed in which it had appeared, it disappeared.

I am safe.

The face of death had just disappeared somehow. I was on the ground but I was still alive. The thread on my wrist was actually doing its thing. Keeping me safe. I scanned my surrounding for more threats and saw two lions facing each other.

"No"

I heard someone say. I searched for the source, but there was no one. May be I had imagined it. May be I was hallucinating. I turned to the lions. The one that had attacked me was growling with anger. Whereas other one, my savior, appeared calm but growling as if giving a warning.

"No"

I heard it again. I was not sure where it came from. I searched around but detected nothing that can speak. I focused myself on lions again. Both beasts were facing each other. The one that had dived in was smaller than the one who was trying to kill me. Both beasts faced each other.

"No"

I heard it for the third time yet I was not sure of where it had come from. I scanned all the direction for any possibility of presence of humans, but there was none.

The beasts growled at each other for moments. The one, which had attacked me, walked towards my savior. Both of them looked into each other's eyes for a moment. Than the lion that had attacked, me backed off and disappeared into the forest. My savior looked at the spot where lion had disappeared for moment, to make sure that other lion had actually gone. Then he turned to me.

He was not as majestic as the lion he had just faced, yet he was larger than any other lion that I had ever seen. He came towards me limping.

I realized it. I had saved the same lion from the clamp. Finally, the decision I had taken the day before had paid off and I was still breathing the fresh air. I stood up and looked around for the knife.

It was missing.

I searched repeatedly for it but could not find it. Then I felt wet in my pants. I looked down and felt ashamed of what I saw. I had peed in my pants. I was so embarrassed that I turned red with shame but I was glad that there was no one here to see me in such a condition.

In order to clean my pants, I walked into the stream and sat down in water. The lion remained standing at his position looking at me. He must be wondering what must be going on with me. Was I crazy or nuts to sit in the stream like that? He would not understand how it felt to pee in the pants on seeing the death. How could he? He was just a dumb animal with no sense and understanding, but I must say they have feelings and gratitude, because after all he was the one who had saved me.

After few minutes, I came out of the water again and stood at the banks. Water dripped from my pants. After a while, the lion started moving.

It walked past me towards the forest. It stopped and turned towards me at the edge. It appeared as if he wanted me to follow. Having no idea about what to do next, I obliged. As soon as he was sure that I was following, it started moving again.

He appeared to be recovering quickly from the injury. After few minutes of walk, he stopped and turned to a tree. It was a neem tree. He raised himself on two legs with support of the trunk, caught hold of one of the branch, and plucked it out. Then he started rubbing his injured leg with the neem leaves.

This animal was not surely dumb. I looked at him with awe. I was not sure, whether animals knew of benefits of neem trees or where by birth provided with knowledge of Ayurveda. Whatever may be the reason; this animal somehow had the intelligence. Otherwise, how can a carnivore know anything about plants? It even had plucked a branch with his mouth, which was made to accept nothing else but meat. Whatever may be the reason behind its intelligence, or whatever it was, I was glad that he was with me and I felt safe in his presence. This must be how Androcles had felt when the lion had saved him.

I plucked some leaves from the tree for myself and rubbed it on the scratches on my chest. It burned but I kept on rubbing.

Once we were done, we resumed our journey. It was amazing to follow him. I had never thought that I would be walking so close to such a majestic animal with its beautiful mane, all bare handed, without any protection. Yet it was there, walking in front of me or may be, guiding me through the forest.

We kept on moving. On some occasion, the lion will stop at some spot and I too will stop there. Sometimes after stop, we will move back from the way we had come and will turn in other direction, which we had left earlier. It appeared as if he had forgotten the path earlier and remembered it all of a sudden.

There was complete silence between us. Sometimes I thought of breaking the silence, but if I talked to him, it was going to be a soliloquy. Therefore, I thought against that thought and remained silent.

All that time when we walked, I thought of the voice that I had heard at the bank of the stream. I was not sure where the voice had come from. May be, someone had come searching for me, or may be someone was passing by and had seen me with two lions and was calling out to me and suggesting me to get away from them. The second time when I heard it, it appeared as if lion was speaking but that is impossible. Animals cannot speak and I know that. It only happens in stories. It must have been illusion or I might be daydreaming, or it may be seeing the death that had made me hear things that did not exist.

No, I was not daydreaming, nor it had been an illusion, someone had spoken then and I will find the out the one who had.

We were walking on the edge of the denser part of the forest. On right hand, there was dense forest of trees and on the left; there was vast open ground of grass. I thought of the movie The Lion King. I imagined Simba roaming in such open field. I thought of the adventures he had in his jungles. I wondered if every lion's life is same. I wondered if the lion who was guiding me had the same life as that of Simba.

"Your life must be full of adventurous no?" I asked without expecting any response.

The lion turned around with confused look on his face but soon he continued with the walk. I was not sure why was I talking to him. He was not going to understand me and even if he does, he is not going to talk to me. Still I kept on talking to him.

"Roaming wherever you wish, killing anything you like. Your life must be amazing." I said.

There was no response from the beast. He kept on walking.

"I wish I could live the same life as yours. I want to live the life the way you do. Do whatever I like. No worries. No Fear. No one to be scared of."

The lion stopped all of the sudden. He looked around as if scanning the surroundings, and from nowhere made new way through the trees. I had no option but to follow him.

"Your life must be luxurious. You have no worries. You have nothing to bother. You can go wherever you like. You can be with anyone you wish to be with."

I took a pause and then again continued with my soliloquy.

"Thank god you intervened or else, right now I would have been in some semi-digested form in his belly. You know I am still not sure whether this is all real or just a trick of my mind. I mean walking with a lion, king of all animals, all alone in a forest, it sounds like a fairy tale. You are guiding me through all this danger, how am I supposed to believe this, and you know what, I even thought that I heard someone shouting 'No...No' when you were trying to protect me back there and...."

All of a sudden, the lion stopped and turned around looking directly into my eyes. I was not sure of what had happened but he kept on staring at me. I stood there paralyzed as the lion kept his eyes focused on me. Again, after few moments, he turned around and kept on walking.

I thought that I saw a light of understanding in his eyes. My heart was saying to me that he understands every single word that I was speaking. He is not just any dumb animal.

"Hey, stop..." I said.

However, the lion continued walking as it should, like a dumb animal.

"Umm..." I continued. "I think I heard you speaking."

The beast stopped on the path. It turned again and stared at me. Not knowing what to make of it, I continued.

"I think I heard you. It must have been you. You had said no to other lion when you had come to my rescue. You were the one whom I had heard and I know you could understand me. You spoke earlier and I know you can speak again. So please say something or at least give me some hint so I can figure things out. There was no one around at that time except for three of us, and the way you just looked at me, I feel like you understand every single word that I speak and yet you are acting dumb in front of me. Speak to me if you understand. Speak if you can or else just give me some hint."

The lion kept on staring at me.

After few moments, it turned, and resumed the journey. No words, no hint, nothing from the beast. I was sure that I was dreaming or I had an illusion. I was a fool to think like that. How can an animal speak? He was just repaying his debt and I was seeing too much in it. That iswhat this is.

Whatever it be, I continued following him. For rest of the journey I kept mum. I was not sure of anything anymore. After few minutes, the grassland on my left disappeared and once again, we were in the dense forest.

After few meters, we stopped. We were at the top of the hill. I walked and stopped next to the lion. I could see the carpet of trees in front of us and in the distance; I saw two different dirt roads merging into one.

I am almost there. There were only few kilometers to cross and then I will be back to the human world. At last my journey through the wilderness was about to end.

"Can you hear me?"

I heard that voice again. It was the lion. The animal that I had thought is dumb, had just spoken to me. I knew it. I was not dreaming. It was not an illusion. He had spoken then, and right now, once again, he had spoken.

"Yes, I could." I replied.

He stood there in silence.

"Was it you who spoke there on the bank of the stream?" I asked.

"Yes."

"Is it really you who is speaking? Please do not tell me that you can speak. Please say no. Please!"

"No. All right! However, it is I. I am the one who is speaking right now and I was the one who had spoken there. The voice you had heard was mine."

I was not sure what to make out from all that was happening right now.

"How can you? I mean you are not supposed to speak. You are supposed to be dumb. Yet you speak. How is that possible?"

"There's a lot hidden behind this trees that humans are not aware of."

"You mean there are others?"

"Yes."

Now many others can speak like him. I wondered how this animal had remained undiscovered until now. Maybe I was the first person who had bumped into a speaking animal.

"Was the lion that attacked me, like you?" I asked

"Yes."

I was amazed as well as stunned that there exist animals who could speak. They exist and yet no one knows about them, and above it, one of them had attacked me.

"Why was he attacking me, or is it like that only and you are just helping me because I had helped you earlier. What is it? I want to know."

"It's because of the thread in your hand. I'm helping you because of that thread."

I looked at the thread that Panditji had tied on my wrist.

"What's going on and what is all this about? Tell me."

"For that, you will have to stop here and now, and join me to the place to which I'll take you."

"Why but?" I asked.

"It's because of the prophecy that we are told. You are no ordinary boy; you are the one that our kind awaits, the chosen one."

"What? Wait how come I am the chosen one?"

"The thread makes you and your past action confirms that."

"You mean peeing in my pants, does that make me the chosen one."

"No. I mean you helping me. Your kindness. That confirms that you are the chosen one."

I thought of all that he had said. He thinks me as someone who is a part of a prophecy, and was asking me to join him, just because of a thread tied to my wrist that again was a result of a broken jar.

This was all just a mistake. Panditji must have mistaken me for someone else and tied me this thread; and this lion had made the same mistake because of this thread now. This mistake had cost me so much. I had almost died in the process.

"What if I refuse to join?" I asked.

"It's your choice. The path to civilization is in front of you. I will escort you until you are safe, and then you can be back to your civilization, but remember that many lives depends upon you. Many lives out there are lived for your existence. If you leave, you take the hopes of many that depends on you."

I thought of his words. I knew it is a mistake and I am not the chosen one. How could I be? I had peed in my pants on seeing the death. Generally, the chosen one in any story is supposed to be brave and strong and that, I certainly was not.

"What if this is all a mistake?" I asked. "What if I am concerned as someone I am not?"

"You are more than what you think you are. And if you are not, you could always get back with your life."

"Fine then. I will meet others." I said. "If I am the chosen one, I'll stay, but if not, you'll get me back to my world, safe."

"They will love to meet you. Perhaps we all are waiting for you. And if you are not the one we are waiting for, I promise, that I will get you out safe and sound."

"Okay then, let's get going." I said.

"Yes. Let's go, but before that, let me inform others about your arrival."

"Wait; don't tell me that you use cell phones."

"No." He said with a smile. "We don't. We have our own ways of communicating."

After that, he turned towards the forest and gave out a loud ear-shattering roar. Another roar soon followed his roar in distance, then another one far, and then another one farther until I could hear nothing at all.

"I think you should use cell phones." I said jokingly.

*

# CHAPTER 10

A bald man with a well-muscled body rushed into the main office of the forest officer. For past many months, he had constantly waited for something unusual to happen. He had no idea of what this was all about, or what he was supposed to look for. He was just asked to keep a watch for occurrence of any unusual event, and after wait of so many months, it finally had occured.

"What is it?" a man with heavy muscles and rowdy moustache asked.

"It's there." Bald man replied. "The unusual thing that you were talking about, it had finally happened."

"What's the unusual thing?"

"There was a series of roars, one after other in the forest."

"What's unusual about it? It could be a mere coincidence."

"It isn't. A boy had disappeared in forest and had not been found yet. The timing of his disappearance and this stream of roars could not be a mere coincidence. There is some connection between this two and we should find it out. If you are still in search for that unusual thing that you are talking about, you should go after this."

"Hmm," the man replied. "Call for the chopper, we need to get inside the forest."

"I already did but there is none available. They are all kind of booked and will take a day before any of the chopper gets free."

"It doesn't matter. Ask the agency to send one as soon as possible."

The bald men nodded to his superior and left the room and the man with the moustache wasall alone again. He had waited for this for so long and it was finally here. After so long time, he thought, he will finally get answers to all his questions.

*

# CHAPTER 11

"So you had been following me all along." I said.

It had started getting dark and we were moving through the dense forest. We were travelling to some place where they all lived together, isolated from human world. I had just learned that he had seen me falling through the waterfall and since then had kept an eye on me. Even the glowing eyes that I had seen in the dark and thought was nothing, was his.

"Then why didn't you came to my rescue, when you saw me falling?" I asked.

"We can't. We are told not to intervene with humans until necessary."

"Then why did you save me from crocodile?"

"You are the chosen one. I had to protect you. Apart from that, if an animal gets the taste of human flesh, they get addicted to it, and we can'tallow that. Therefore, I had to keep them away from you. And apart from that, you had saved my life, so I had to save yours."

"Hmmm. It explains why I had no encounters with any of the animals yet. You must be the one who kept them out of my way. Wasn't it you?"

"Yeah. I kept them away from you. And even when we had started moving toward your human world, we would have bumped into some, if we hadn't changed our path from time to time."

"That's why you stopped now and then. I should have figured it out."

"Yes. You should have, but you did not. Guruji always said humans can easily be diverted, and that's what happened to you."

"Yeah. So who is this you call as Guruji? The immortal king?" I asked remembering what Panditji had said about meeting the immortal king.

"Yes, but for us, he is Guru. We walk on the path he leads us on, and we do what he commands us to do. We are what we are all because of him, and if not for him, we would not be there. He had taught us many things, for a purpose, that we have to serve, and till the day until the purpose is fulfilled, we are dutiful to him."

"What is it that purpose that you are supposed to fulfil?"

"Let's stop for now. Go and Get something to eat for you. We will pass the night here. There's a lot we need to discuss and you need to learn a lot along with not peeing in the pants."

I gave a fake smile to him and then started looking for anything that can satiate the mice in my belly.

For so long, humans had considered themselves superior than other species. The power of learning and thinking had made our race evolve and civilize into society. We created great monuments and civilizations with power of our mind and for decades, they had stood to represent our superiority over other species. However now, the facts of superiority are going to change. These animals are smart and superior in all way. In case of strength, they obviously are superior. In case of smartness, some humans might outsmart this lion, but what if the other lions are smarter than him and this one is dumbest of all. Whatever may be, humans would have to soon, think twice before saying that humans are the most intelligent species. They are about to have a superior competition.

Anyways, I searched for fruits on trees and got few mangoes for myself. Once I had plenty, I walked back to lion. From there, we walked to a water point nearby, that forest department had built for animals. After that, we settled down under a neem tree.

"Can I rest my head on your back? If you don't mind." I asked.

"No. You can't." he replied.

"Why can't I?"

"Because I don't want you to. You need to find something else for your support."

"Why are you being so mean? You could help me with some comfort and where in the hell am I supposed to find pillow and blanket in this jungle?"

"I don't know and what do you expect from a wild animal? We are supposed to kill you, and eat you. You cannot expect comfort from someone who is superior to you! Go get whatever you can for your comfort and get some sleep."

"Aren't you supposed to take care of the chosen one?"

"Nope! Not actually! We are just supposed to protect you!"

"Fine then. Good Night."

"Good Night and sweet dreams!"

I managed to rest under a tree close to him. I closed my eyes feeling the cool air of summer. It was cold and I felt my body shiver. I thought of the events of the day and the fact that there exist animals that can speak like humans. I thought about the lion and although he was being jerk, I felt relieved that he was with me. My thoughts flowed from him to jungle to events that took place during the day. Soon I lost track of time and was fast asleep until the moment when I again opened my eyes.

\*

Next day I woke early. I found myself sleeping with the lion. It must have been a cold night and he might have covered me to keep me warm. At last, he had shown some kindness despite of all arguments he was making with me. He was still sleeping and I decided to let him sleep and give him as much rest as possible. Therefore, without making a noise, I got up and walked to the water point. I washed my face and drank few gulps of water from it.

When I was about to leave, I heard a movement. I turned around and searched for the source, but located nothing. Again came the noise. I turned around and saw a leopard on the other side of the water point. It had its eyes on me. It was slowly making its way to me. I felt fear run through my spine. I wanted to cry for help. I wanted to cry for the lion, but I doubted if I would be alive to let out the scream. I had seen on the discovery how fast leopards could move. I stood there as it made its way towards me taking all the time in the world.

However, all of a sudden it stopped. I heard a low angry growl coming next from me. It was the lion. I haven't even heard him coming. The leopard stood there for moments and then quietly disappeared into the forest.

"Don't go anywhere without me." said the lion.

"Okay." I replied.

He walked in front of me and suddenly turned and looked at my trousers.

"Thank god you haven't spoiled your trousers. Because I haven't got any." He commented.

I smiled. Although his comment should have made me angry or ashamed, I felt relieved that he was with me.

"I would have spoiled my trousers if you wouldn't have been there. I don't know how you animals manage such a scary stare on others."

"You think he stared at you because he wanted to scare you?" he asked

"What other reason could be there? I am an easy prey for him. Bare handed, how am I supposed to protect myself against him. He got all those teeth and claws to his advantage to finish my game. And all he had to do was just scare me a bit and then kill me."

"He wasn't scaring you. Actually he was scared of you."

"You must be kidding. He and scared of me. Why would he be scared of me?"

"Think it like him. Wouldn't you be scared of human if you are an animal and you see a human in the forest?"

"I can't think like him and why should he be scared of a human being in a forest? Humans have roamed for centuries in the jungle."

"…and killed infinite number of animals of which many already got extinct and many are on the verge of."

"But how am I supposed to be a threat to him. I don't even have a weapon...wait...what is this."

I took out the knife that hung on my belt. It had not been there before, yet it was there now. I had no idea where it came from but I again had a weapon for my protection.

"Where did this come from?" I asked him.

"You had it when I met you and you saved me with it earlier. Don't you remember?"

"No. I mean Yes, I do, but I had lost it earlier when the other lion had attacked me. Since then, it was not there with me."

"It was. You must had some other thoughts because since the moment we had been together, this knife had always been there with you."

"Okay. It might have slipped out of my mind."

"Yeah. You see now why he was scared of you. Any living being will be scared of you if you roam in the forest with that thing."

"Sorry! I had almost forgotten about this thing. By the way thanks for saving me for the third time."

"There's nothing new in that. Your race is coward when it comes one on one?"

"Yeah, yeah, someday I will repay your debts."

"I'll be waiting for that day."

He walked to the water point and drank water from it. Once he had filled himself, he came to me.

"Shall we continue then?" he asked.

"Sure. But what about my breakfast?"

"We will have it on the way. Now start moving."

We continued marching towards the uncertain location. We left the dense forest and entered the grassland. On the way, we plucked some fruits from the trees.

"Won't you have anything for yourself?" I asked him.

"We can go without food for fifteen days and without water for four days, but I'm not going to extend my hunger for that long. I already got my meal with me."

"You do?" I asked him with a surprise. "Where is it?"

"Oh boy! Why do you keep forgetting yourself?" he said.

"Ah, don't tell me you are taking me with you as your lunch. You are supposed to protect me."

"Obviously not. I am not going to let you live for that long. You are my breakfast."

I stopped on my way. This kind of jokes, I don't like.

"Very funny! Ha-ha! I laughed on it. Fine now. Now if you want to go for hunt, you please move on because my mind won't allow me to join a hungry lion."

"Oh, don't take it seriously, I was just kidding. Anyway, I got breakfast along with me when you plucked those fruits, and it is not you. Just throw me some fruits."

"You must be kidding."

"I'm not. Will you pass me the fruits or should I grab it on my own along with some of your flesh!"

"Wait-Wait! Take this."

I threw some mangoes to him and he grabbed it in mid-air. In seconds, he threw out the remains on the ground. I kept looking at him in total amazement.

"You are a vegetarian?" I asked very bewildered

"Not actually. But we sometimes go vegetarian."

"Why sometimes?"

"We are carnivore and we need flesh, but Guruji is taking us to new food practice. He says we need to learn to survive without meat. It might help in upcoming situation."

"And what is that situation?"

"You will learn that soon."

I walked along with him. I was not sure of what to make out of all these things. I was walking with a lion to certain unknown location. Above it, the lion who was speaking to me, was acting jerk now and then, and never missed a chance on commenting on me and as if that all was not enough, he was a vegetarian. A carnivore that consumed an herbivore as a food was a vegetarian. I laughed out in amazement.

"Why are you laughing?" He asked.

"Nothing."

"You are gone mad."

"Yeah! I too think so! Anyway, so what greater purpose do you serve?" I asked.

"It's long story." He replied.

"We have all the time in the world."

"Are you sure you want to hear it?" he asked. "It will bore you."

"Yeah! I'm sure."

"Fine then. Tell me how much do you know about Mahabharata"

"Nothing much. I only know that there were five Pandavas and hundred Kauravas and both of them fought at Kurukshetra and in war Pandavas won."

"And what do you know about Yadavas, Satrajit, Ugrasen, Balarama, and Krishna?"

"I know about Lord Krishna and his brother Balarama and have somewhere heard about Yadavas, but nothing about the other guys."

"Hugh. You call yourselves superior and intelligent. You don't even know about your scriptures."

"Now please don't start it again. If you are so intelligent then why don't you tell me?"

"Yeah! I do know. I was wrong. Whom was I asking? Anyway, let me tell you a bit. I know you will not understand this all but you will have to hear it all. If not from me, now, than from the Guruji himself, later. You are supposed to know it all and this is all from the scriptures."

"Okay." I said not knowing what was this all about.

"This starts from King Nahushake in tenth chapter of fourth part of

Vishnu Puran..." he started. "...King Nahushake had six children. Yati, Yayaati, Sanyati, Aayati, Viyati, and Kruti."

I looked at him puzzled and amazed. Ever since I had met him, I was discovering new and amazing things.

"Can you repeat the names please?"

"Yati, Yayaati, Sanyati, Aayati, Viyati, and Kruti. The eldest of them was Yati who was the heir to the throne, but he had no desire of the throne. Hence the throne was passed on to Yayaati, who was second eldest of them."

"Sorry to interrupt but can you repeat the name of the king?" I asked.

"King Nahushake"

"...and where does it start?"

"In tenth chapter of fourth part of Vishnu Puran." He replied emphasizing on every single word.

"Wow...if you appear for history's paper, you will definitely score full marks."

"Shut up. Humans are supposed to have knowledge of their scriptures, but you all have lost your mind and have no value for them."

"What good will it do? Who could remember all the dates, when Akbar was born, when war was fought, when this had happened, when that had happened, why remember all that is nonsense? Why remember that which had already passed? It is the future that one should think about, not the past."

"You need to know the past because it holds your future, because your past tells you the mistakes that your ancestors have made that you shouldn't, because your history is base for your present."

"But how can one remember all the dates?"

"You shouldn't remember the dates. It is the knowledge of your past that is important. How much history is taught, does not matter? How is your history taught is what matters. History is the stories that already had taken place. It should be told as the story, not as facts, and everyone knows that it is easy to remember stories than facts. Then why make it difficult. Remember, every future needs a history to build upon. The person who don't know history of his nation is......umm. I forgot rest of the lines"

"Ha...ha...! That was quite a line."

"Don't laugh! That sometimes happen to me but I still remember many great thoughts about history."

"Oh really! Can you speak them for me?"

"Sure...Umm...

This is by Edmund Burke, 'Those who don't know the History are destined to repeat it.'

Then this is by Malcolm X, 'History is a people's memory, and without a memory, man is demoted to the lower animals.'

Then this is by Rudyard Kipling, 'If history were taught in the form of stories, it would never be forgotten.'

Then this is by Anon, 'If the lessons of history teach us anything, it is that nobody learns the lessons that history teaches us.'

Then this is by Norman Mailer, 'It is not the sentiments of men which make the history, but their actions.'

And then…"

"Wait-Wait, that's enough for me. I am not going to remember even one from them. You better save it for someone else who can remember it."

"That's the problem with humans. You do not value the wealth you have in books. Anyway who am I to judge you all?"

"Yeah! Who are you to judge us? I am the chosen one and you are not. Anyway what happened to the Prince Khyati?"

"It's not Khyati! It's Yayaati."

"Whatever! So what happened next?"

"So Prince Yayaati was entitled as the next king. He became the king and got married to Sukracharya's daughter, Devyani, and Vrushaparva's daughter Sarmistha."

"So unlucky man" I said.

"Why unlucky man?"

"Can't you see? He got two wives. Generally, man is married to one woman only as a punishment, but king Yayaati had to marry two. So double punishment. Poor king. I feel sorry for him."

"Very nice of you to think so much about the king. Now shut up and listen. Queen Devyani gave birth to two sons named Yadu and Turvarshu and queen Sarmistha gave birth to three named Duhayumn, Anu, and Puru."

"Hmmm. Five more names to remember. Where did you learned all this from?"

"By reading the scriptures."

"You mean you can read books?"

"Yes. Why?"

"Nothing. It just all sounds like fairy tale. I get stuck in a jungle and meet a lion who is about to kill me and all of a sudden another lion comes in and saves me and then it comes out that this lion can talk, and above it, the lion is a vegetarian and as if all this fact were not enough, another surprising facts comes out that the lion can read. I don't know what surprises lies ahead in front of me? I wonder if you can write or not?"

"Obviously not. Can you visualise our claws holding pencils and pens? Ha. That will look so funny. If it's about typing then we have not yet tried it but I'm sure we can manage that but writing, no, that's not possible."

"How come you know so much about human world and scriptures and…wait you also know about computers, that means you are in contact with human world, Is that so?"

"Yes! You should have figured it out earlier when I talked about species getting extinct and humans beings scared of lizards and man-eaters and what not. But you are so ignorant that you can't make out things looking at the facts that are in front of you."

"Yeah! Yeah! Whatever! So what happened next in the Khyati's Story?"

"Yayaati. Not Khyati. King Yayaati. He got five babies from two wives. Yadu, Turv…"

"Please skip that part. Those names will not fit in my head. So please continue with story."

"Yeah! Better skip names for your less capable mind. So next, father-in law of king Yayaati, Sukracharyaji cursed him for some reason, and due to Sukracharya's curse, Yayaati met old age at very young age. Later when Sukracharyaji got delighted on king, he told him that he could exchange his old age with his son. When king Yayaati asked his elder son Yadu to give his youth for thousand years so that he could enjoy the pleasures of the youth, Yadu refused. As a result, he cursed Yadu that his son will not be capable to be heir of the throne.

Again, he asked Turvarshu, Duhayumn, and Anu for their youth. All of them refused and as a result, king cursed them all. In the end Sarmistha's youngest son Puru agreed and king Yayaati exchanged his old age with Puru for his youth."

"Wow!" I said, "At that time, it was a fashion to curse someone. First Sukracharyaji cursed Yayaati, Yayaati cursed Yadu, Yayaati cursed all his children, and in Mahabharata Draupadi cursed Duryodhan, and so on. Why do they curse so much earlier? Hmm?"

"Ummm…Actually I don't have answer to that question. It never occurred to me."

"Here's one thing why we humans are superior to you all. We think of what we listen and we question what we do not understand. Got it? You do not understand the things. You just listen to what you hear."

"If that was the case then it won't have been possible for me to remember so many things. We too do understand what we are told. However, our questions are logical. We don't ask questions like fools."

"So you are not going to lose your side that easily. No problem. I will too stick to my side and give you solid reasons until you accept that we are superior. Now please continue with the story."

"I'll see who accepts and who makes the other accept. Anyway, on getting young once again, king Yayaati started enjoying the pleasures of the youth. While enjoying pleasures with his wives, he thought that he would satisfy and end all the pleasures that he had thought of. With such thoughts, the king's pleasures were never satiated and hence remained in constant arousal. As a result, thousand years passed and his need for pleasures kept on increasing and his pleasures never got satiated."

"Yeah, lust never satiates. The more you try to satisfy the lust, the more lustful you get."

"On realizing of his greed for the pleasures he returned the youth to Puru. He disclaimed from the throne and went into the forest. Before leaving, he appointed Turvarshu on south-east, Duhayumn in west, Yadu in south, Anu in north and Puru as the king of the throne.

From here, we do not need to worry about all other descendants of king Yayaati. The only descendant that we need to know about is the eldest one, Yadu.

The descendants of the eldest son of king Yayaati are known as Yadavas. This lineage of Yadavas had given many great men to India. One of which was Arjun who had earned many boons in his life. One of them was, one thousand hands due to which he was also known as Sahastraarjun. In his kingdom, nothing ever got destroyed."

"Wait! Wait! Wait! I know this person Sahastraarjun. My mom used to tell me stories and it was one of them. I remember the story. This guy had stopped flow of a river and then...ummm..."

I scratched my head in order to remember what the original story was. I had heard it for so many times from my mother but still I could not remember it.

"Is this what you call remembering? Shall I narrate it?"

I nodded not surprised that he knew this story too.

"Once, Sahastraarjun was playing in Narmada river wearing his Vaijayantee Mala. At that time, he stopped the flow of Narmada river by spreading his thousand arms. Ten-headed Raavan was also there nearby. He came there with the desire of having a fight with Arjun, but he found this place very beautiful, so he started worshipping Lord Neelkanth there on the shore of Narmada.

When Arjun stopped Narmada water with his thousand arms, river started flowing backwards and Raavan, who was worshipping there, got disturbed. His worship materials flowed away in backward flow of Narmada, his tents etc. floated over that water. Raavan considered himself very mighty, so he could not tolerate this. He went there and said some bad words to him. Then Sahastrabaahu – which is again one of the name of Arjun, caught him in his arms and kept him as captive in capital of his kingdom, Mahishmatee Puree.

Later when Maharshi Pulastya, who was grandfather of Raavan, heard about this, he himself came to Arjun. Arjun welcomed him and politely asked –

'What can I do for you?'

Maharshi Pulastya said –

'I accept your bravery, but this is my grandson, so free him.'

Arjun respected him and freed Raavan. He even gave him divine clothes and jewelry and extended his friendship to him too.

This is how the story ran. Remember it now?"

"Yeah, but my mother used to narrate the story in much better way than you do."

"Used to?"

"She is no more."

"I'm sorry. I didn't know that."

"It's ok. Does your mother narrate stories to you?"

"Yeah! She used to."

"Why used to?"

"She too is gone."

"I'm sorry. I should have understood."

"It's fine. Let's continue with the story."

I noticed how he changed the topic of his mother. He too, like me does not want to talk about it, and I too, do not like forcing. After all, I will not like people forcing me on things that I do not want to speak. This thing was common between us that we like keeping things to ourselves.

"With help of boons he ruled for eighty-five thousand years." He said. "In the end he was killed by Lord Parashuram which again was one of the boon in which he had asked to get death from the person who is famous in all the three worlds."

"Hmmm! That is very long time to rule. Now a day, government doesn't even work properly for five years."

"Yeah I have read about it, but we got consistent government in our state. Gujarat is developing under his guidance."

"Yeah! Narendra Modi! All credit goes to him"

"Hmm! I have heard conditions of other states. Although I haven't visited another state, and obviously I can't, it is said that Gujarat is much safer to live in than the other ones."

"Yeah! I know, but from where do you get all this news? Who connects you to the human world?"

"You would learn soon when time comes. Now let us move back to the story and remind me whenever we switch on other topic from our story. We are switching over the topics too frequently and it's all because of you."

"What's my fault in that?"

"It's all your fault and stop asking questions now. So where were we?"

"Dying from someone who is famous in all three worlds."

"Yeah I know. Therefore, Sahastraarjun was killed by Lord Parashuram which again was one of the boon in which he had asked to get death from the person who is famous in all the three worlds. That I have already said. Now another descendant of Yadu, which we need to know about, is Satrajit. This is where our main movie starts. Until now, it was highlight, or introduction, or base line, or whatever you say in movies.

According to thirteenth chapter of fourth part of Vishnu Puran, Satrajit was the son of Nighna. He also had a brother named Prasena. You need to remember this names."

"I got it. Satrajit, son of Nagina and his brother named Shivsena."

"Oh god! It's not Nagina, its Nighna, forget her, remember Prasena. Not Shivsena, Prasena."

"Got it! Satrajit and Pra…, Prasena…Prasena"

"Remember it by heart."

"Wrote it in my heart! Satrajit and Prasena, Satrajit and Prasena…"

I spelled out the names several time. Once the lion was sure that I had mesmerized the names, he continued with the story.

"So Satrajit was the son of Nighna and he had a brother named Prasena. Now the divine Aditya, the sun god, was the friend of Satrajit.

One day, while walking on the seashore, he addressed Aditya in his mind and hymned his praises. Hearing the call, sun god appeared in front of Satrajit. Beholding the bright and indistinct shape of Aditya, Satrajit said to Aditya

'O lord, I have seen you in the sky, as a globe of fire which restricts my vision to see real form of yours, and now in front of me your brightness does the same. So O lord, please do me a favour and please show me your real form.'

On hearing the request of Satrajit, sun god took off a gem called Symantaka, off from his neck, and with the removal of the jewel, Satrajit saw real form of the sun god, in which he was of a dwarfish stature, with a body like a burnished copper and his eyes, slightly reddish.

Seeing the real form of the god, Satrajit offered adorations to sun god and once he had offered his adorations, the sun god asked him to demand a boon that he wish. As a boon, Satrajit asked that the Symantaka gem becomes his.

On hearing the wish, the sun god presented the Symantaka gem to the Satrajit and then returned to his place in the sky."

"Wow!" I said. I looked up at the sky and raised my hand towards the sun.

"Oh lord of the sky, I have seen you in the sky, every day I see you and bear your scorching heat, but still I never complained to you. Your brightness sometimes blacks out my vision but still I have never complained to you. You see how much am I devoted to you. So oh shining globe of fire, oh divine god, I want to be your friend. Please appear in front of me!"

Nothing happened. I stood like that for moment and again turned back to the lion.

"What was that?" he asked.

"Oh that! I was seeing whether the son god listens to me and whether I can consider him as my friend. I was checking whether he appears on my call or not?"

"And did he appear?"

"Nope. You saw it all and still asking me the question?"

"What if he would have appeared in front of you?"

"Obviously, I would have asked him to show his real form and then when he would have asked me for the boon, I would have asked him for the Symantaka gem like Satrajit."

"And then what?" he asked.

"After that? After that nothing. I would have kept it with me and showed it to my friend on returning back to the human civilization."

He shook his head as if saying no and laughed at god knows what.

"What?" I asked puzzled from his reaction.

"Nothing." He said. "Let's get back to the story. Therefore, Satrajit got Symantaka gem, which is considered as gem of gems, from Aditya. Having obtained the spotless gem of gems, Satrajit wore it on neck and the very moment he had placed the precious gem around his neck, he became as brilliant as sun god himself, and started shining brightly like a sun. Irradiating the entire region with his splendor, he then returned to the city of Dwarka, where Lord Krishna resided.

On returning to Dwarka, the inhabitants of the city, seeing a brilliant form approaching, repaired to the eternal male, Purushottam, who, to sustain the burden of the earth had assumed a mortal form as Krishna, and said to him

'Lord, assuredly the divine sun god, Aditya, is coming to visit you.'

But Krishna smiled, and said

'It's not the divine sun, Aditya, but Satrajit, to whom Aditya has presented the Symantaka gem, which, he now wears. So go and behold him without apprehension.'"

"Hmmm! So this is about the time when lord Krishna was alive."

"Yes. Therefore, after hearing the lord, they all, the inhabitants of the city, departed. On returning to Dwarka, Satrajit retired to his house, and deposited the Symantaka gem in his house. Symantaka gem yielded daily eight loads of gold, and through its marvelous virtue, dispelled all fear of portents, wild beasts, fire, robbers, and famine.

You see how powerful this gem is. And you wanted to have it so that you can show it to your friend."

"Ok. That is why you were laughing. I had no idea of magical powers of the gems so I use that part of story to lighten up the mind, and, how was I even supposed to know about that. You hadn't told me about its power earlier."

"You started before I could complete, and something needs to be told only when the time is right. Else it won't hold much importance and it won't have as much effect as it is meant to have."

"Fine then. Have it your way. Now please continue."

"Ok. Therefore, Satrajit deposited the gem and the gem with its magical powers, gave him the gold and kept all fears, famines, and all other things, away from him. Now Lord Achyuta was of opinion that this wonderful gem should be in the possession of Ugrasen; but although he had the power of taking it from Satrajit, he did not deprive him of it. He thought that this might occasionally generate disagreement amongst the family. Satrajit, on the other hand, fearing that Krishna would ask him for the jewel, transferred it to his brother Prasena."

"Wait! Wait!" I interrupted. "Now who is this new characters now? Who is Achyuta and who is Ugrasen?"

"Achyuta is one of the name of Lord Krishna, which I thought you must be knowing and Ugrasen, according to my knowledge is his uncle, more precisely he was one of the two son of king Ahuk, you don't need to remember his name. He had a brother named, Devak, again, whose name you don't need to remember. Devak had a daughter named Devaki, who was married to King Vasudeva and gave us Lord Krishna. Now don't tell me you don't know about Devaki and Vasudeva?"

"Obviously! I do. Every Hindu knows about them and parents of Lord Ram. So in relation Ugrasen was Lord Krishna's Uncle and King of Mathura and father of Kansa."

"King of Mathura, Yes, but father of Kansa, we could say that theoretically but actually it wasn't so."

"What? He wasn't son of Ugrasen?"

"Kansa is believed to be Ugrasen's son, but actually, he was born to Ugrasen's wife and a Gandharva named Dramila. Once, in her youth, Ugrasen's wife was walking in the forests with her house cleaners when Dramila saw her and impregnated her. She got furious of it and said that since Dramila had made her pregnant using devious means, a child born of her husband's clan would kill Dramila's child. Then as time passed, Kansa imprisoned Ugrasen and took over the kingdom and then lord Krishna came, killed Kansa, freed Ugrasen, and gave him the kingdom and as lord Krishna was son of Devaki, he was from clan of Ugrasen and Kansa was from the clan of Dramila. So in the end, Ugrasen's wife's words came true and a child from her husband's clan killed the child from her and Dramila."

"My god! I'm totally getting confused."

"You don't need to remember everything. Just focus on the story. Forget rest all the things."

"Ok then. Continue with the story."

"So, it was opinion of lord Krishna that this precious gem should be with his uncle, Ugrasen, but in order to avoid disputes in the family, never bought up the matter. On other hand, Satrajit, thinking that, lord Krishna will snatch away the gem from him, gave the gem to Prasena.

Now it was the peculiar property of this jewel, that although it was an inexhaustible source of good to a virtuous person, yet when worn by a man of bad character it can be the cause of the person's death.

Now as the Prasena had the gems of gem with him, he once hung it round his neck, mounted over his horse, and then went to the woods to hunt. While he was hunting, a lion chased him and in the chase, he was killed. The lion, taking the jewel in his mouth, was about to depart, when he was observed and killed by Jambavat, the king of the bears. I assume that you know the king of bears, King Jambavat."

"Yes I do. He was there with lord Ram when he was fighting against the devil king, Raavan."

"And?" he asked.

"And what? That's all."

"You need to improve your knowledge about your religion. You lack a lot. Anyway, listen to this carefully, because king Jambavat is the main pillar in all of this."

"Carry on." I said.

"Jambavat is a first form of humans created by the creator of worlds, Lord Brahma, with lots of hair on his body. He is perhaps not a bear but we all have seen him like a bear only. He is described as monkey in many scriptures but that cannot be true of what we know. He is immortal to all but Lord Vishnu.

Jambavat was present at the churning of the ocean, and is supposed to have circled lord Vamana seven times when he was acquiring three worlds from Mahabali. He is said to be present during all the incarnations of god.

He is the king of Himalayas and have received the boon from Lord Rama that he would have a long life, be handsome and would have the strength of ten million lions"

"Is that all?" I asked tired of listening to the long list of achievements of the king of bears.

"No. There's a lot but I won't say it because you are not interested in it."

"Of course, I'm interested, but in story, not in the facts that I can't remember."

"Ok then, let's move back to the story. So when the lion was about to leave with the gem, King Jambavat killed the lion and took the charge of the Symantaka gem.

King Jambavat carried off the gem and retired into his cave. He gave the precious Symantaka gem to his son Sukumara to play with.

On the other side, when some time had elapsed, and Prasena did not appear, the Yadavas began to whisper one to another, and to say,

'This is Krishna's doing, desirous of the jewel, and not obtaining it; he has perpetrated the murder of Prasena in order to get it into his possession.'

When these calumnious rumours came to the knowledge of Lord Krishna, he collected a number of the Yadavas, and accompanied them to pursue the course of Prasena by the impressions of Prasena's horse's hoofs. Ascertaining by this means that a lion had killed him and his horse, he was acquitted by all the people of any share in his death.

But Lord had the desire to recover the gem so, he, with others, followed the steps of the lion, and at no great distance came to the place where the lion had been killed by the bear. Following the footmarks of the king Jambavat, he arrived at the foot of a mountain, where he asked all other Yadavas to await him, while he continued with the track.

Still guided by the marks of the feet, he discovered a cavern, and had scarcely entered it when he heard the nurse of Sukumara saying to him,

'The lion killed Prasena; the lion has been killed by Jambavat. Don't weep, Sukumara, the Symantaka is your own.'

Thus assured of his object, Lord Krishna advanced into the cavern, and saw the brilliant jewel in the hands of the nurse, who was giving it as a plaything to Sukumara. The nurse soon descried his approach, and marking his eyes fixed upon the gem with eager desire, called loudly for help.

Hearing her cries, Jambavat, full of anger, came to the cave, and a conflict ensued between him and Achyuta, which lasted twenty-one days. The Yadavas who had accompanied the latter waited seven or eight days in expectation of his return, but as the foe of Madhu, didn't appeared for so many days, they concluded that he must have met his death in the cavern.

They thought that,

'It could not have required so many days, to overcome an enemy.'

Therefore assuming that lord had died, they departed, returned to Dwarka, and announced that Lord Krishna had been killed. When the relatives of Achyuta heard this intelligence, they performed all the obsequial and ceremonial rites suited to the occasion.

The food and water was thus offered to Lord Krishna in the celebration of his Shraddha, served to support his life, and invigorate his strength in the combat in which he was engaged; on the other hand, his adversary, wearied by daily conflict with a powerful foe, bruised and battered in every limb by heavy blows, and enfeebled by want of food, had no more strength to fight him. Overcome by his mighty antagonist, Jambavat cast himself before him and said,

'You, mighty being, are surely invincible by all the demons, and by the spirits of heaven, earth, or hell; much less are you invincible by powerless creatures in a human shape; and still less by such as we are, who are born of brute origin. Undoubtedly you are a portion of my sovereign Lord Narayan, the defender of the universe.'

Thus addressed by Jambavat, Lord Krishna explained to him fully that he had descended to take upon himself, the burden of the earth, and free the world from all the devils that had developed during all the years of his absence. The Lord Krishna kindly alleviated the bodily pain suffered by the king of Himalayas, from the fight, by merely touching him with his hand. Jambavat again prostrated himself before Krishna, and presented to him his daughter Jambavati, as an offering suitable to a guest. He also delivered to his visitor, the Symantaka jewel. Although a gift from such an individual was not fit for his acceptance, yet Krishna accepted the gem for the purpose of clearing his reputation."

"Hmmm." I said.

I had never involved myself so deep in Hindu stories. They were amazing as well as complicated but carried so much with it that it could tell so many things to humans and provide solutions to many of their problems. But now a days, we are forgetting the values of this scriptures. I too was one of them because until now, I had not thought of all this, but today I was learning and listening to stories from the scriptures from an animal.

"That's all for now. We will continue the story after a while."

I looked up at the sky, towards the sun. It was just above the head. That means it was already noon. I wondered where all the time had passed. The story had consumed the time and I have enjoyed it. Although I still do not remember any of the names or facts, but still it felt nice to hear a story from someone.

"What now?" I asked.

"It's lunch time. Then we will take rest and after having the rest, we will again start marching."

"Fine then. Where's lunch?"

"You need to get that."

"Why me?"

"Because I'm the king of the forest, and it is your duty to serve me. Now go and get something for me to eat."

He took shelter under one of the tree while I stared at him. He was a total jerk.

"What?" he asked.

"You are not serious. Are you?"

"Sure I am."

"You see this?" he asked bringing out his paws and showing off the claws.

I gave in the argument and started searching for the food.

"Actually Lions could not climb trees so you will have to bring more and more." He cried out.

"Lions are also not meant to speak so please keep mum." I said.

I picked up some fruits from trees and piled it in front of him. Then again, I searched and collected more fruits and added it to the already diminishing pile.

"Can't you wait?" I asked.

"Wait for what?" he questioned me back.

"Wait for me. We could have lunch together."

"Why would I take lunch with you? You are not my date nor are you a king, and we kings, got some standards to maintain. Now stop wasting the time and bring some more fruits."

I left him again in search for more fruits frustrated with his behavior, but I was enjoying the frustration.

"He is going to make me mad." I said to myself and laughed all alone at that.

Once I had collected more than enough fruits for me, I went back to him. By that time, he had already finished the pile and was relaxing like a king. Yes, like a king. He was acting as if he was a king.

"You finished with your belly?" I asked.

"Yes. But if you are offering more, than I have no problem in that."

"No, No! This all is for me now. Can I use you as support for my back?"

"No. I am sorry. I got to maintain some standards."

I ignored him, sat down next to him, and relaxed my back on his belly. He jerked his body few times to shoo me away but I held my position. In the end, he gave in and I relaxed myself on him. I kept all the fruits down and then closed my eyes and picked one of the fruit and started eating it. I enjoyed the fruit eating session.

One after other, fruits started disappearing down my stomach but it wasn't only my stomach that was consuming the fruits. Lion was also sharing the fruits that I had bought for me. I have not realized it until the moment, when I extended my hand for a fruit and was sure enough that there should be few more left for me, but what my hand found was nothing.

"Thief!" I said. "How dare you eat my part of the lunch?"

He laughed at me.

"Your name wasn't written on them. I found those fruits on the ground and as there was no sign of its owner, I made it my property and consumed it down."

"Liar! You knew that those were mine and still ate them. You did that to harass me. But you listen, I'm not going to get harassed. Keep those fruits. I don't need them. I am full. Someday, you will also remember that some great man had given you a food to eat. You owe me a debt of piles of fruits."

"Whatever!" he said.

After that, I closed my eyes and relaxed myself for the noon nap. When I opened my eyes again, the lion was already awake. I did not ask whether he had taken a nap or not, because I knew that I am definitely not going to get a straight reply for any of my questions.

We again continued with the journey to the unknown location and he resumed the story from the place where he had left.

"So Lord Krishna got married to Jambavati and accepted the Symantaka jewel for the purpose of clearing his reputation He then returned along with his bride Jambavati to Dwarka. When the people of Dwarka beheld Krishna alive and returned, they were filled with delight. All those who were weak in health too bowed down to the lord with newfound youth. All the Yadavas, men and women, assembled around Anakadundubhi, the father of the hero, and congratulated him.

Krishna related to the whole assembly of the Yadavas all that had happened, exactly as it had befallen, and restoring the Symantaka jewel to Satrajit to exonerate himself from the crime of which he had been falsely accused. He then led Jambavati into the inner apartments.

When Satrajit reflected that he had been the cause of the aspersions upon Krishna's character, he felt alarmed, and to conciliate the prince, gave him his daughter, Satyabhama, as a wife.

"Wow! Another wife! Really, Lord Krishna was so unlucky..."

"You again started with your nonsense. Keep mum!" he said.

"Yes my lord." I said.

"So Lord Krishna was married to Satyabhama. But before the marriage, Satyabhama had been sought in marriage by several of the most distinguished Yadavas, as Akrura, Kritavarman and Satadhanwan."

"So here come new characters. Please carry on because I know I'm not going to remember any of those names."

"Ha-ha! I know that already. So Akrura, Kritavarman and Satadhanwan were highly incensed at her being wedded to another, and leagued in enmity against Satrajit. The chief amongst them, with Akrura and Kritavarman, said to Satadhanwan,

'This caitiff Satrajit has offered a gross insult to you, as well as to us who solicited his daughter, by giving her to Krishna. Let him not live. Why don't you kill him, and take the jewel? Should Achyuta therefore enter into feud with you, we will take part on your side.'

Upon this promise, Satadhanwan undertook to slay Satrajit.

Meanwhile, when news arrived that the sons of Pandu had been burned in the house of wax, Krishna, who knew the real truth, set off for Barannavata to allay the animosity of Duryodhana, and to perform the duties his relationship required."

"Wait-Wait!" I stopped him.

"Isn't this burning the wax house episode, part of Mahabharata?" I asked.

"Yes it is but you must remember, my dear, that all this happened during the life of Lord Krishna, and as Lord Krishna was present at the time of Mahabharata, characters of Mahabharata are also part in the life of this story, directly or indirectly."

"My god! It is getting more and more complicated. Anyway, please continue with the story."

"So Satadhanwan taking advantage of Lord Krishna's absence, killed Satrajit in his sleep, and took possession of the gem, Symantaka.

When this came to the knowledge of Satyabhama, she immediately mounted her chariot, and repaired to Barannavata. Filled with fury of her father's murder, she told her husband how Satrajit had been killed by Satadhanwan in resentment of her having been married to another, and how he had carried off the jewel. She implored him to take prompt measures to avenge such heinous wrong. Krishna, who is ever internally placid, being informed of these transactions, said to Satyabhama, as his eyes flashed with indignation,

'These are indeed audacious injuries, but I will not submit to them from so vile a wretch. They must assail the tree, who would kill the birds that have built their nests. Dismiss excessive sorrow; it needs not your lamentations to excite any wrath.'

Returning back to Dwarka, Krishna took Baladeva apart, and said to

161

him,

'A lion slew Prasena, hunting in the forests; and now Satrajit has been murdered by Satadhanwan. As both these are removed, the jewel which belonged to them is our common right. Up then, ascend your chariot, and put Satadhanwan to death.'

Being thus excited by his brother, Balarama engaged resolutely in the enterprise; but Satadhanwan, being aware of their hostile designs, repaired to Kritavarman, and asked for his assistance. Kritavarman, however, declined to assist him, pleading his inability to engage in a conflict with both Baladeva and Krishna. Satadhanwan thus disappointed, applied to Akrura; but he said,

'You must have recourse to some other protector. How should I be able to defend you? There is no one even amongst the immortals, whose praises are celebrated throughout the universe, who is capable of contending with the wielder of the discus, at the stamp of whose foot the three worlds tremble; whose hand makes the wives of the Asuras, widows, whose weapons no host, however mighty, can resist. No one is capable of encountering the wielder of the ploughshare, who annihilates the prowess of his enemies by the glances of his eyes, that roll with the joys of wine; and whose vast ploughshare manifests his might, by seizing and exterminating the most formidable foes.'

'Since this is the case,' replied Satadhanwan, 'and you are unable to assist me, at least accept and take care of this jewel.'

'I will do so,' answered Akrura, 'if you promise that even in the last extremity you will not divulge its being in my possession.'

To this Satadhanwan agreed, and Akrura took the jewel; and the former mounting a very swift mare, one that could travel a hundred leagues a day, fled from Dwarka.

When Krishna heard of Satadhanwan's flight, he harnessed his four horses, Saivya, Sugriva, Meghapushpa, and Balahaka, to his chariot, and, accompanied by Balarama, set off in pursuit."

"Was it necessary to name those horses?" I asked.

"No, it wasn't, but I like to see the look on your face whenever some new character is introduced. You should look at yourself! You look funny!"

"Oh! Thanks for the compliment." I said.

He totally ignored me. He was enjoying his own comments on me.

"Now please continue!" I said getting pissed off.

"So..." Continued the lion, barely controlling his laughter. "...the mare held her speed, and accomplished her hundred leagues; but when she reached the country of Mithila, her strength was exhausted, and she dropped down and died. Satadhanwan dismounting, continued his flight on foot. When his pursuers came to the place where the mare had perished, Krishna said to Balarama,

'Do you remain in the chariot, while I follow the villain on foot, and put him to death; the ground here is bad; and the horses will not be able to drag the chariot across it.'

Balarama accordingly stayed with the chariot, and Krishna followed Satadhanwan on foot. When he had chased him for two Kos – which is around four miles, he discharged his discus, and, although Satadhanwan was at a considerable distance, the weapon struck off his head. Krishna then coining up, searched his body and his dress for the Symantaka jewel, but found it nowhere. He then returned to Balabhadra, and told him that they had effected the death of Satadhanwan to no purpose, for the precious gem, the quintessence of all worlds, was not upon his possession.

When Balabhadra heard this, he flew into a violent rage, and said to Krishna,

'Shame light upon you, to be so much greedy of wealth! I acknowledge no brotherhood with you. Here lies my path. Go where you please; I have done with Dwarka, with you, and with our entire house. It is of no use to seek to impose upon me with your perjuries.'

Thus reviling his brother, who fruitlessly endeavoured to appease him, Balabhadra went to the city of Videha, where Janaka received him hospitably, and there he remained."

"Wait! You mean, Baladeva left Lord Krishna?" I asked.

It was surprising to me that Baladeva had left Lord Krishna. In every story I had heard about Lord Krishna and Mahabharata, they stood next to each other. However, for first time, I was introduced to other chapters in which their paths were separate.

"Yes!" he replied.

"I had never heard any stories like that from anyone! What happened next?"

"So Baladeva went to Mithila and Vasudeva returned to Dwarka. It was during his stay in the dwelling of Janaka that Duryodhana, the son of Dhritarashtra, learned from Balabhadra the art of fighting with the mace.

At the expiration of three years, Ugrasena and other chiefs of the Yadavas, being satisfied that Krishna had no jewel, went to Videha, and removed Balabhadra's suspicions, and brought him home.

Now coming back to Symantaka Gem, Akrura, carefully considering the treasures, which the precious jewel secured to him, constantly celebrated religious rites, and, purified with holy prayers, lived in affluence for fifty-two years; and through the virtue of that gem, there was no dearth nor pestilence in the whole country.

At the end of that period, Satrughna, the great grandson of Satwata, was killed by the Bhojas, and as they were in bonds of alliance with Akrura, he accompanied them in their flight from Dwarka. From the moment of his departure various calamities, portents, snakes, dearth, plague, and the like, began to prevail.

On this occurrence, all those whose emblem is Garuda, called together the Yadavas, with Balabhadra and Ugrasena, recommended them to consider how it was that so many prodigies should have occurred at the same time. On this, Andhaka, one of the elders of the Yadu race, thus spoke,

'Wherever Swaphalka, the father of Akrura, dwelt, there famine, plague, dearth, and other visitations were unknown. Once when there was want of rain in the kingdom of Kasiraja, Swaphalka was brought there, and immediately there fell rain from the heavens.

It happened also that the queen of Kasiraja conceived, and was quick with a daughter; but when the time of delivery arrived, the child issued not from the womb. Twelve years passed away, and still the girl was unborn. Then Kasiraja spoke to the child, and said,

'Daughter, why is your birth thus delayed? Come forth; I desire to behold you, why do you inflict this protracted suffering upon your mother?'

Thus addressed, the infant answered,

'If, father, you will present a cow every day to the Brahmans, I shall at the end of three years more be born.'

The king accordingly presented daily a cow to the Brahmans, and at the end of three years the damsel came into the world. Her father called her Gandini, and he subsequently gave her to Swaphalka, when he came to his palace for his benefit. Gandini, as long as she lived, gave a cow to the Brahmans every day. Akrura was her Son by Swaphalka, and his birth therefore proceeds from a combination of uncommon excellence. When a person such as he is, is absent from us, it is likely that famine, pestilence, and prodigies should fail to occur? Let him then be invited to return: the faults of men of exalted worth must not be too severely scrutinized.'

Agreeably to the advice of Andhaka the elder, the Yadavas sent a mission, headed by Kesava, Ugrasena, and Balabhadra, to assure Akrura that no notice would be taken of any irregularity committed by him; and having satisfied him that he was in no danger, they brought him back to Dwarka."

"Wait, Wait, Wait!" I said. "What was this all? Everything passed above my head. Can you explain it in simple words?"

"Yeah! Why not! But from where did you missed the track?"

"From where Symantaka Gem was reintroduced in the story." I said.

"Okay! So in simple language, in the story, Akrura is said to have lived with Gem for fifty two years. As long as he had the gem, there never occurred any dearth or famine or anything like that in the nation. Till now clear?"

"Yes."

"So, now comes a turn in a story. One of the allies of Akrura, dies in a battle with a Bhojas. Therefore, Akrura had to accompany his alley in the flight from Dwarka. The very moment, Akrura left Dwarka with the Symantaka Gem, bad things started happening in the Dwarka. Various calamities, portents, snakes, dearth, plague, and things like that, began to prevail. All this time, Symantaka Gem had protected the land, but now when the Gem was gone, all of these things had come at time. Do you get everything till now?"

"Yes! Carry on."

"So on seeing so many prodigies at a same time, the Yadavas, with Balabhadra and Ugrasena, held a council to talk upon the matter. In this council, Andhaka, one of the elders of the Yadu race, told them that it was all because of Akrura's absence that these prodigies were occurring. He told the Yadavas that Akrura was a great person and his presence had kept all these prodigies out of the country's boundary, but now, when he is gone, the power that was protecting the land is gone and so all these things were occurring."

"Now how come this Akrura been considered as a great person? I don't understand it at all!"

"Leave it aside! You will not understand it. It is a story in this story. You only need to remember that he is considered as a great person and they thought that it was Akrura's powers that was keeping all these prodigies at boundaries.

Is everything clear till now?"

"Yes!"

"Okay now as the Yadavas were convinced that the reason behind the occurrence of all these prodigies is Akrura's flight, they sent a team to bring Akrura back to Dwarka. Is that all clear or need more explanation?"

"No! It is fine! Move Ahead!" I said.

"So when Akrura returned to Dwarka, immediately on his arrival, in consequence of the properties of the jewel, the plague, dearth, famine, and every other calamity and portent, ceased.

Krishna, observing this, reflected that the descent of Akrura from Gandini and Swaphalka, was a cause, was wholly disproportionate. He wondered what it could be that his arrival had all those things out of the kingdom and his absence had made them prevail.

'Of a surety,' he said to himself, 'the great Symantaka jewel is in his keeping, for such I have heard are amongst its properties. This Akrura too has been lately celebrating sacrifice after sacrifice; his own means are insufficient for such expenses; it is beyond a doubt that he has the jewel.'

Having come to this conclusion, he called a meeting of all the Yadavas at his house, under the pretext of some festive celebration. When they were all seated, and the purpose of their assembling had been explained, and the business accomplished, Krishna entered into conversation with Akrura, and, after laughing and joking, said to him,

'Kinsman, you are a very prince in your liberality; but we know very well that the precious jewel which was stolen by Satadhanwan was delivered by him to you, and is now in your possession, to the great benefit of this kingdom. So let it remain; we all derive advantage from its virtues. But Balabhadra suspects that I have it, and therefore, out of kindness to me, show it to the assembly.'

When Akrura, who had the jewel with him, was thus taxed, he hesitated what he should do.

'If I deny that I have the jewel,' thought he, 'they will search me in person, and find the gem hidden amongst my clothes. I cannot submit to a search.'

So reflecting, Akrura said to Narayan, the cause of the whole world,

'It is true that the Symantaka jewel was entrusted to me by Satadhanwan, when he went from hence. I expected every day that you would ask me for it, and with much inconvenience therefore I have kept it until now. The charge of it has subjected me to so much anxiety, that I have been incapable of enjoying any pleasure, and have never known a moment's ease. Afraid that you would think me unfit to retain possession of a jewel so essential to the welfare of the kingdom, I forbore to mention to you it's being in my hands; but now take it yourself, and give the care of it to whom you please.'

Having thus spoken, Akrura drew forth from his garments a small gold box, and took from it, the jewel. On displaying it to the assembly of the Yadavas, the whole chamber where they sat was illuminated by its radiance.

'This,' said Akrura, 'is the Symantaka gem, which was consigned to me by Satadhanwan: let him, to whom it belongs, now take it.'

When the Yadavas beheld the jewel, they were filled with astonishment, and loudly expressed their delight. Balabhadra immediately claimed the jewel as his property jointly with Achyuta, as formerly agreed upon; while Satyabhama, demanded it as her right, as it had originally belonged to her father. Between these two Krishna considered himself as an ox between the two wheels of a cart, and thus spoke to Akrura in the presence of all the Yadavas:

'This jewel has been exhibited to the assembly in order to clear my reputation; it is the joint right of Balabhadra and myself, and is the patrimonial inheritance of Satyabhama. However, this jewel, to be of advantage to the whole kingdom, should be taken charge of by a person who leads a life of perpetual continence: if worn by an impure individual, it will be the cause of his death. Now as I have sixteen thousand wives, I am not qualified to have the care of it. It is not likely that Satyabhama will agree to the conditions that would entitle her to the possession of the jewel; and as to Balabhadra, he is too much addicted to wine and the pleasures of sense to lead a life of self-denial. We are therefore out of the question, and all the Yadavas,

Balabhadra, Satyabhama, and myself, request you, most bountiful Akrura, to retain the care of the jewel, as you have done hitherto, for the general good; for you are qualified to have the keeping of it, and in your hands it has been productive of benefit to the country. You must not decline compliance with our request.'

Akrura, thus urged, accepted the jewel, and thereafter wore it publicly round his neck, where it shone with dazzling brightness; and Akrura moved about like the sun, wearing a garland of light.

After that Symantaka Gem is never mentioned in Vishnu Puran or any other scripture."

"So? Is this all that I need to know from Vishnu Puran?"

"Yes!"

I grasped all that he had said until now. I looked at the sky, which had already started getting dark. On the edges, sky was starting to turn orange. I took in the scene. I imagined the incidents that lion had just narrated to me.

"But I don't understand how it explains your existence and great purpose you exist. You said that once I had known the story, I would know the reason behind your existence. But I can't make out anything out of your story." I said.

"For that you need to know what happened to Symantaka gem after that." Said Lion.

"But how am I supposed to know that if none of the hindu scriptures mentions what happened later." I asked.

"I'll tell you. It was during the period when Krishna knew his time of incarnation is over.

Lord Krishna visited his father in law, king Jambavat. At that time, he presented the Symantaka Gem to the Jambavat and asked him to keep it out of reach of humans. Since that day Jambavat had protected the Symantaka Mani. Until some hundred years ago he realised that his time on this world is about to get over and he is soon to attain Moksha. But before he attains the ultimate salvation, he will have to pass on the gem to some protective hands which will keep the gem, out of the mortal world's reach.

Therefore, since the day, he had learned that his time for salvation is due; he had searched for someone who could take care of the Symantaka gem. For years he searched, but could not find anyone and decided that he alone could not search him. Then he started teaching animals and converted them from just mere wild animals to intellectual living beings. He taught all these animals about the Hindu scriptures. He made them strong. He taught them discipline, and at the end told them about the purpose for which they were converted.

Since then animals are searching for any human who appears them to be different from others. Who, if acknowledged by the king of Himalayas, will be the chosen one for the protection of the gem."

"It means that there are other animals too, like lions, who could talk and Symantaka gem still exist."

"Yes and no. Symantaka gem does exist but talking animals doesn't."

"But how is this possible?" I asked. "You're talking with me and I could clearly hear you."

"Yes we do, however, not in the way that humans could understand. Only the chosen ones will have the power to understand our methodology of tongue. And as you're the chosen one, it's your gift from the god who had sent you to the aid for the salvation of the king, and our guru."

"I understand that king Jambavant is your guru, but how come the existence of gem possible? I mean, if the gem still existed, there will have been no draughts and calamities and prodigies in the country. But now a day, every single day, new prodigy and disaster and calamity is taking place!"

"I don't have the answer to those questions."

"Then who does?"

"Maybe, King of Himalayas can answer your question."

"You mean King Jambavat?" I asked.

"Yes."

"Hmmm! Can you show me the Symantaka Gem?"

"We can't show it to anyone unless King Jambavat permits. In fact, not all of us have seen the gem. Only King Jambavat, and his close one's knows the whereabouts of Symantaka Gem."

It was so confusing. I looked at the lion and then at my surroundings. We stood at top of a hill, and in the distance, I saw few more hills. Behind the hills, sun was about to disappear completely. The sky behind the hills was in complete shade of orange, giving a mesmerizing view to the eyes.

"That's where the council meets." Lion said. "There at the foot of those hills. That is where we need to go."

We started climbing down the hill. The journey downward was faster than that of climbing.

"Can I ask you few things?" I asked.

"Yeah!" he said.

"Was the lion that attacked me like you?"

"Yes! Why?"

"I heard you speaking to him. That means he understands you. And if he understands you than it means he is intellectual. Right?"

"Right!"

"Then why was he after me. I mean, if he is also intellectual like you, wouldn't your goal and his goal be the same? After all, you are all made for common goal. Search for the chosen one and protect him."

"Yes! Our goal is same. However, the story behind the attack is very long. I will tell you sometime later."

"Don't tell me all, but at least, tell me something. I want to know."

"Fine then. I do not know it all but few years back his son was killed by a train and since that day, he had lost trust in humans and always gets angry when he sees them. That is why he is kept in those regions where there are no human activities. He kills every human he sees, roaming in forest. Maybe someday his anger will calm and he will see humans in the way he should."

We were almost to the foot of the hills where the councils of lion held. We were walking towards the hill and it had already started getting dark.

"Hi Kesari!" came voice from the trees on my right.

I turned at the source and saw a lion approaching us from the trees. He was shorter than the lion next to me.

"Hi Sambha!" said the lion standing next to me.

"You got names? Why didn't you tell me?" I asked.

"You never asked." Kesari replied.

"It appears you haven't said few things to him." Said Sambha.

"Just what he had asked for and what matters to him right now."

"Then he got a lot to learn. Anyway, council is waiting for your arrival. It appears he is not afraid of us, anymore. I don't want him there if he is scared."

"No need to worry. He is the chosen one and is brave enough to meet the council."

"Fine then. Let's go."

Saying it, Sambha started walking and we followed him to what was supposed to be the council of lions.

*

# CHAPTER 12

We followed Sambha through the trees. He was guiding us to the council. Kesari, who also knew the path, was behind me. So in between both this lions, I felt like a special guest who was about to enter a hall, full of lions, who were eagerly waiting to meet me.

After few minutes, Sambha stopped at one place and asked me to wait until he was back. Kesari came and stood next to me. Sambha went ahead, disappeared behind the trees and after few more minutes, came back. He asked me to follow him.

After few steps, we entered a cave in one of the hill. Few steps later, it got dark and then few more steps and we came out of the cave into a clearing.

It was not how I expected it to be. I had visualized the council gathering like those shown in Ramanand Sagar's Ramayana. However, what I saw was completely different.

Here there were at least around twenty to fifty lions and lioness seating in a wide circle. One lion who was even larger than Kesari was standing. There was absolute silence. Everyone was listening to the standing lion who was addressing them. Our entry in the hall caused the distraction that made all the heads in the room, with and without mane, turn to us.

"Welcome Kesari." Said the lion who was standing. "I would like to hear what you have to say. We are running out of time."

"Yes my chief."

Then Kesari narrated all that happened from the day since I had been thrown from the waterfall. He skipped few things like me peeing in my pants and getting scared. I was glad that he had not said those things in front of everyone. It took few minutes for Kesari to narrate all that had happened to the council.

"From what my son Kesari had told us," said the lion that was standing, "...it appears that you are the one whom we had searched for years."

First, I missed the point on hearing that Kesari was the son of chief, which means he will be the next leader of the tribe. I bowed my head low and said to the chief.

"I don't know anything about that, but I'm ready to help you and meet the great bear, king Jambavat, and be to your service in any manner in which I can." I said.

"I am Singh, chief of this tribe. On behalf of all I welcome you and until the day, king of bears himself declares that you are the one, you are our guest. All the lions and lionesses you see here, were out in the search for you, and with announcement of your arrival, all of them had returned back to their home, to welcome you, who we hope, would be declared as the chosen one. On behalf of Guruka, who is right now on a task to accomplish, and who had attacked you, I ask you to forgive him and accept our apologies."

On the mention of the name of the lion who had attacked me, I noticed that the lioness who was seating third on the right of the chief saw down.

"There is no need for apologies, my lord. It would be honor for me to stay with you all."

"Kesari," said the chief to the Kesari. "Take our guest with you and show our quarters and make sure of the arrangements for his dinner."

"At your command, my lord."

We left the council and moved to the hills. These hills had different caves. Kesari told me that this caves were their main quarters. They all live in this when they are all together. However, generally, all the lions are scattered in the forest so that they can search for the chosen one. Right now as they have considered me as the one, they all were there except for Guruka and few others. He told me that he had conveyed the message to their source, in human world to stop the search here and now, as the chosen one had arrived to their aid.

Once Kesari had shown me the quarters, we moved to the forest for the dinner, which would obviously be fresh fruits. On the way, Sambha accompanied us. We walked through the trees. After few meters in the forest we came to a point where we were surrounded by all kinds of fruits.

"You can have whatever you like." Said Kesari.

I did not require any more invitation. I was hungry and there was so much there for me to eat that could last for lifetime. I climbed trees and ate the fruits until my mouth and stomach refused to accept any more. It was already dark but it was full moon and there was enough light for me to see the things. We started walking back towards the quarters.

"What task is Guruka assigned?" I asked Sambha.

177

"He is gone to the east." Sambha said.

"For animals in this forest," he continued, "most dangerous place is east. That is the area where most poachers have their camps. Many times, we also get caught, but Makata, the monkey, had always helped the lions to escape. At night, he unlocks the cages and free us, whenever we get caught. He has one of the naughtiest and craziest bunch of followers after him. He and his gang is always there to help us, but right now, he had disappeared somewhere.

Seven of the Lions that were in east who should have been here by yesterday night have not arrived yet. They have not responded to the calls that we had made to them. So, we had tried to contact Makata, the monkey. We failed in contacting him too. There was no reply from his side. We asked other monkeys for help but they were of no use without their leader.

From all this, it appears as if they are captured or killed. Whatever the reason, chief had sent Guruka to investigate in the morning. We expect him to return by night."

"What if he doesn't arrive?" I asked.

"We all except kids and few of the lioness, will move to find the cause and rescue the captured ones, if they are alive!" answered Kesari.

"Do these poachers know anything about you or gems?" I asked.

"No. They don't know anything. Although few times we had discovered few poachers treading near our camps which were unusual, but till date we had never met anyone who appeared to know anything about us."

I compiled all that I had heard. I tried to map if there could be any connection between the gem and poachers, but the answer was no. Kesari was confident about that, and I have not heard anything about that until now from anywhere. This group of poachers might be here for animal skins and bones. I somewhat now understood how much troubled life this animals lived.

Once we had reached to the caves, Sambha left us, from there, Kesari and I, went to his father's cave. At the entrance, Singh appeared. I bowed my head to him as a sign of respect.

"Would you like to have leaves-bed arranged for you?" Singh asked.

"No. there's no need for it." I said. "I have seen worse."

Singh looked lost in thoughts, and from what appeared to me, he was looking at something in distance. We stood there in complete silence for moments. When I felt uncomfortable of the silence, I decided to initiate the conversation.

"So you all will be marching in the morning for rescue?" I asked.

To my question, he kept his gaze fixed on something in distance.

"It appears you have learned a bit about us." He said after a while. "Yes. We will start the march in the morning, but you and Kesari will stay here along with other lionesses and cubs. After all, we cannot risk the life of the chosen one, for whom, we had searched for years."

"I understand your highness." I said, "I don't want to be of any trouble to you, and so will stay back with the others, but I suggest you to take your son with you. His bravery could be of use if there are any complications in the situation."

Singh smiled at me. He remained silent for few moments and then spoke.

"After long period of time, someone had used the word bravery for my son. I appreciate that but he is supposed to be here, with you. It is his duty to stay with you until Guruji is back, and as my son, if anything happens to me, he has to take care of the tribe in my absence. Therefore, he too, will remain with you and wait till we are back."

He again focused his gaze somewhere and got lost in thoughts. After few moments, Singh moved to the corner of the cave and retired. We too retired in another corner of the cave. I sat next to Kesari taking his back as a support.

"May I ask you a question, Kesari?" I asked.

"Yes." He said.

"Why did your father said that after long period of time someone had used the word bravery in your context?"

He remained silent to my question. He sat there without saying anything. I too sat in silence without pressuring or forcing him to say anything. After few moments, he answered.

"It's a long story." He replied.

"I would like to hear it." I said.

He hesitated in the beginning of whether to say it or not but in the end he decided to share the story with me and he finally started with his story.

"Few months ago, my mother and I were in south east corner of the forest, searching for the chosen one. We were walking along the bank of a stream, when all of a sudden, I do not know how, my mom was caught in a clamp that was laid down by the poachers. I had no idea of what to do at that moment so I tried to free her with my claws and jaws. With all my strength, and all the possible techniques that I knew, I tried to free her, but I failed in freeing her from that clamp. I tried repeatedly but my every effort was in vain. The clamp was tight. I stood there with her and started thinking of a way to get her out of it, but nothing came to my mind. Panic took over me and I was on the verge of tears.

Then all of a sudden, we heard voices from the trees. It was from the poachers, and they were closing rapidly.

My mother asked me to run away. I protested but she forced me. I stood there as tears ran down from my eyes. How can I leave her all alone in danger? I stood there. My mother asked me repeatedly but I refused to leave her. If I left her all alone in the hands of poachers, she will be as good as dead, but if I stood there with her, at least there was the chance that I could fight the poachers and save her from them. She said that it is not an appropriate thing to do, and asked me to leave. However, I again refused to obey her and so she made me swear on her name and forced me, against my will, to leave her all alone in the danger.

I had no other option but to obey her and so, I ran away from her against my will. That was the last time I ever saw her.

As I ran, poachers shot me with their guns, but I was too fast for them to aim. In the end, I was out of the danger, unharmed, but still broken.

When I returned to my father and told him of everything that had happened, he, Guruka, few others, and I immediately rushed to the spot where I had last seen her. She was not there. She was gone and the only thing that said that she had been there were drops of her blood. My father got angry on me for leaving her. All of them called me coward for running away. I did not say anything to them of how my mother had forced me to leave against my will. I just stood there, and accepted whatever they said. I was a coward. I had left my mother to die in the hands of the poachers. She is no more in this world now and it was because of me. If I had stood there with her, and fought against those poachers, she might have been alive, but no, I left, and she is no more now.

When all of us returned back, I told my father everything that had happened there. I told him of my protest and her pleas and how I finally ran away against my will. He listened to it all, and once I had told him everything and cried for our loss, he apologized for being angry on me.

However, not everyone knew of the incidents that had occurred back then and considered me as coward. Since that day, every day, they call me a coward. Every time, when there is a danger on us, they ask me to remain back with kids and other lionesses. They say I am not brave enough to fight against anyone. And today also, they doubted if I had made a mistake in recognizing you as the one, for whom we had searched for all this days.

Sometime I wish I had died that day and not my mother. Every single day since that day, I regret the decision I had taken. If only I had not obeyed my mother that day, this all would not have happened. However, sometimes, fate plays a cruel game. I do not know about others, but for me, it surely had. I wish I could undo that day.

All that had happened in the past will stay with me and I could not change it. Now I need to live with it. That is the punishment for me for leaving my mother alone. I am a coward and that is to stay with me forever. There is nothing I could do now."

We sat there in silence. I was not sure of what to say. I was speechless. Kesari had just opened up to me and narrated the worst things of his life.

"I am sorry for your mother." I said. "But I don't think you are a coward. You stood for me against Guruka, who was mightier than you were. Yet you forced him to surrender. That is what I call bravery."

"It isn't." He objected. "It was what anyone would have done. That is our duty and is a part of our purpose."

"No. It wasn't." I said. "Do you think any other lion would have stopped Guruka? No. No one would have ever dared to stop him. It requires guts to stand against someone like Guruka and you did. You stood against him for me. That makes you different from others. That makes you braver than others and you did the right thing that day. You had no other option but to obey your mother. It needs very strong heart to follow what your mother says in such a situation. And even a stronger heart to accept those brutal comments, when nothing they thought about you, was correct."

"That's nice of you to say," He said "but for me, and for all other lions, I was a coward then and I'm a coward now."

We sat there in silence after that. I thought of what he had just said to me. I felt sorry for him. For his loss. And reason for his loss was my kind. Humans had ruined life of Guruka and Kesari. And yet we considered ourselves superior than others. I now see how much inferior we were against this animals.

"I think our kind have done too much unfair things to you all." I said.

"We took away your mother from you. We took away Guruka's kid. We took many other things that I do not even know. Yet none of you ever complained, and above it, you saved me. Not once but twice. I have no idea of how I will repay the debt that I owe to you, but, I promise you that I will do everything I could to help you. To help every animal."

I thought of what I said. I was not sure why I said the things I said but I was glad that I did it. I was no different from the others who had taken away the loved ones from Kesari and Guruka.

"I'm sorry, Kesari." I said again.

"It's okay. You had no part in any of this, and you saved my life, even before you knew any of these. That is what makes you the chosen one. Not this prophecy nor this thread, it's your actions that matters."

I nodded. I promised myself that I will do everything to help them and will not break their trust. If, on being an animal, they could show so much of understanding, then god had given my soul a body of human for a reason. I need to have humanity in me and should have better understanding then them. This was chance; not only for me but also for my race to show that humanity was still out in this world, and that, should begin with correcting what my kind had done wrong with them.

"Will you take me to Guruka's wife?" I asked.

"Why?" he asked in response.

"I want to apologies to her for what my kind had done to her family."

"Sure." He replied.

We left the cave in silence. We started walking to the right side. After few steps we stopped. In front of us was another cave. Kesari entered the cave and called out in low voice for Guruka's wife.

"Nrushikaji…"

"Yes. Who's it?" Came the reply from the cave.

"It's Kesari. Shiv wants to talk to you."

After few moments, a shadow of lioness appeared from the dark.

"Yes. What's it?" she asked.

"Can we talk somewhere else?" I asked. "I don't want to disturb others."

"Sure." She said.

We walked away from the caves into the forest. We stopped when we were far enough from the caves for someone to hear. All of us sat there facing the moon. Moonlight illuminated the beautiful form of creature that sat next to me. Kesari's mane shined in moon light and he looked like some godly animal that had come down on earth to enjoy and roam in the forest.

"Hmm...I don't know how to say it..." I started with hesitation.

"Simple. Just say it without hesitation." Said Nrushikaji with a smile.

"Umm...I...I...I just want to apologize you for what my kind had done to your family." I said.

"You don't need to apologize." She said.

"No. I do. I need to apologize. Our kind had been too unfair to you all. I do not know how it feels to lose a son, but I do know the pain of loss. I had once, loved someone, sincerely, and felt the pain when she had left. I had fought with my best friends and felt the pain when they had left. I had lost my loved ones too and felt the pain. That pain is what I am here to apologies for. The pain that my kind had bought upon you.

From the very day, when I had lost my parents, I had wished to change what had happened to them and undo the past to bring them back. It still sometime is hard for me to believe the loss that had already occurred, and I had no one to blame for my loss except for the god. Maybe, the time for my parent's death had come and it was time for them to rest in peace. Nothing could have changed that, but, in your case, your loss was untimely. Your loved ones were taken away from you before time. They died before their time was due, and the one who did it was my kind. You had every right to blame us. Your husband had every right to kill me there. Your kind had every right to hurt us. Yet, you all treated us with respect. You never harmed us, and still, we keep harming you.

That is why I must apologize. I know I could not fill the loss of your son, but I promise I would do all that I could to stop the things that are harming you all. That is the least I could do after all the wrongs we have done to you."

I was not sure of how it sounded to them, but I had made up my mind to help them. Nrushikaji said nothing to me and I too expected nothing from her. This was unexpected, even for myself. I had not thought of apology that I was asking for right now. Every word that I spoke was unplanned. The only thing that I knew right now was that, we had done injustice to them and somehow we need to change things now.

"Kesari," Nrushikaji said, "…would you leave us alone for few minutes?"

"Sure." He said.

He stood up and disappeared into the darkness of the forest. Once he was gone, Nrushikaji sat in silence for few moments and then continued.

"Do you know how my son died?" she asked.

"No" I replied.

"Would you listen to it, if I told you?" she asked.

"Yes"

"Hmmm." She said.

"I have not said these things to anyone," she started, ", yet, with you, it feels appropriate. You want to help us and for me that is more than enough. I am not sure whether I am doing right thing or not but it feels right to me. And that is why I'm telling you this."

She paused for a moment and then started again.

"It was early in september three years ago. My husband and I were sent to north-east part of the forest for the search. It was the place where only experienced amongst us were sent, and, as my husband was the most experienced and trusted by the Singh, he sent my husband there. I was allowed to accompany him and as kids always lived with parents in the jungle, they too had accompanied us.

That day, we were walking on, what humans call as railway tracks, and had reached to your so-called railway station. This was not new spot for us. We had been there many times and we knew how trains worked. Therefore, we kept distance from it and took seat in the grass from where we could keep eye on station. We started looking in different directions and searched for any unusual things. That was what we usually did.

It was then that I saw a kid on track. No one knew what that kid was doing on the track, and no one appeared to care for that. All of a sudden, horn of the train honked at the distance and the engine of the train appeared. It was moving rapidly towards the kid. The distance between the kid and the engine was too short. None of your kind could have travelled fast enough to save the kid.

At that moment, seeing the death approaching the kid and no chance of rescue from humans, my husband sprinted in the direction as fast as he could and in final moment, just before the train was about to run over the kid, he saved the kid from the death. Once the train had finally stopped, my husband dropped him and came back to us. He was angry on humans for beings so careless and complained to me for their stupidity. He complained that none of our kind with such signs were possible suits for the chosen one. I smiled at him and felt proud of him for what he had just done.

Later when there was no one at station, and there was no use for us to sit there, we started our journey back to the quarters.

It was on the way that we were taking the rest and the kids were playing.

While playing they had moved on the tracks. They played there without any fear and we too did not thought of it much, as there was no sign of any trains, and there was no schedule of train at that time.

Yet, all of a sudden, a train appeared. It was moving too fast for its limits. Fear overtook us. My husband and I started running for the kids at the same time. Against the speed and strength of my husband, I was left behind. By the time he had reached the tracks, train was already about to crush the kids, but somehow he managed to pick our younger son in his jaws and dived out of the track. Unfortunately, I was too slow and the train crushed our elder kid.

On one side, I stood watching in horror, death of my son and on other side, stood the father who had saved one of his son but failed to protect the other. We kept on looking at the tracks, hoping that somehow, our kid will come out alive, but that never happened. Nothing can escape the death.

When train had passed, we saw the most horrible scene of our life. I cannot even describe the scene that I had witnessed there. We stood there looking at what was remains of our kid. My husband got angry of the thing that your kind had done and so ran after the train. However, the train was too fast for him. I called after him, but he kept on running after the train. I stood there crying with my kid who was now silent, not knowing what had fallen upon us, all of a sudden. We stood there waiting for another train to run over us and kill us. But that train never came. We sat there at remains of our kid, crying. We moaned there for hours until Singh had sent a group to search for us.

Singh bought us back to the quarters and mourned the death of our kid. Mristhikaji, Kesari's mother, also stood there for us.

After that day, my husband hated humans. The day he had saved a human kid from death, human killed his kid. It filled rage in his heart against humans. He said to others that one day all of them would run after humans, when they will see how evil they are. Since that day, he loses his mind on seeing a human and tries to kill every human he sees.

I'm sorry you had to face his anger without any reason."

I had no words in my mind to speak. Deep inside, I felt guilty. Although it was not my fault but still somehow it made me guilty. After all, it was my kind, humans, who had killed the kid. If only the driver had honked, maybe kid would have heard it and moved out of the track and would have been alive, but no, our kind is too lazy to honk to save a life.

After few moments I asked, "Don't you feel rage against humans?"

"I did in the beginning." She said. "But soon I focused on the good things I had with me. It was not actually me, but king of bears who asked me to do it, and miraculously it lessened my grief. I focused on my younger kid and it made me happy seeing him play. However, my husband never came out of the rage. He was constantly angry and as a result, he was always sent in the locations where there were minimum possibility of human existence. He was never the same that he had once been."

A tear rolled down from her eyes. I washed her tears away.

"I'm sorry for your loss. I wish I could change the things and bring you back the husband you once had." I said.

She smiled at me.

"Yes I will. After all I too wouldn't like to see those claws of your husband, every time I see him." I said to lighten the mood.

She smiled as a result. We sat there in silence. I wondered how she might have felt back then.

"You said you lost your parents. If you wish, you could consider me as your mother. After all, I too miss a son I once had. You could fill that gap." She said.

I looked at her and considered what she had said. She was asking me to be her son. To be the son he had lost. In return, she was giving me the parents, which I had lost before long time.

"Thanks." I said and wrapped my arm around her, filling in all the emptiness, that I had felt all these years for my mother.

Tears of joy rolled down from my eyes. After few moments, I took my arms back and we sat there in silence. Nrushikaji had a son now and I had a mother. It felt as if a link to joy that I had missed all this years was coming back to me.

Kesari arrived and stood there puzzled seeing Nrushikaji, and me smiling. After few moments, he asked.

"Am I missing something?"

"No. Nothing." I replied.

"Let's get back to the caves. It's already late." Nrushikaji said.

"Yes." Kesari said.

We went back to the caves. Reaching the caves Nrushikaji returned to her cave and Kesari and I returned to Singh's. As soon as we settled down in the cave, I closed my eyes to sleep. I felt happy because I had mother now and it kind of felt light at heart. I thought of the day that had just passed. The images of the events of the days were flipping through like a filmstrip, in my head, and I was about get a good sleep when Kesari interrupted the flow of my thoughts.

"Hey Shiv?" he was whispering. "Are you awake?"

"I wouldn't be if you hadn't called me. What is it?"

"You said something about loving someone back there," he said

"Yes, I did, why?"

"Nothing. I just wanted to know about it. Would you tell me something more about it?"

"No. But why do you want to know more about it."

"Nothing, it's just that, if you talk with me about it, I wanted an advice from you."

"What advice?"

"It's personal. A story for a story. If you share, I share."

"Ok." I said.

"So?" he asked. "Share it?"

I thought about it for a moment.

"Let's do it. A story for a story."

"Let's do it." He said. "Ladies first."

I looked at him and then we both laughed. It was a story time and we were going to share some personal stories.

*

# CHAPTER 13

We were in silence for past fifteen minutes. I had told Kesari how my and Vaishavi's love story had ended before it had even begun. I told him how I had tried to commit suicide and how Vimal had saved me. I told him how I had moved to boarding school and how I had ended up all alone. I told him everything from my suicide attempts in hostel, to her letter, and then to my parent's death. I had cried heavily, while narrating the story and during all that time, Kesari had remained silent and allowed me to cry it all out.

We walked out of the cave and were in open, when I continued with my story. I told him everything from my school passing, to my first dull college life. I told him how the nightmares had returned to my life and how I was holding myself back. He was listening to every word that I was speaking. Then I told him how my dull life got colors in it with new friends in my second college life. I told him about my newfound love, how I had proposed to her, how I had spent my later days in complete joy with her. I described to him about the days in our college, bunking of the lectures, our hangouts, outings, picnics, everything that we had shared together.

"That's quite a story." He said once I was finished.

"Yeah! I know." I said. "So tell me your story now."

To that, he remained silent. He was reconsidering his decision of telling me his story. When he remained silent for few more seconds, I spoke.

"You can trust me with your story. You know my story and I trust you with it. In same way, I want you to trust me and share your story."

"My story isn't that interesting," He said.

"It doesn't matter," I said. ", just start speaking."

"Okay then," he said, "it is not interesting like yours, but like yours, it is also a love story."

"Aha. See, there it gets interesting." I said and gave him a teasing smile. "Who's the lucky one?"

"I'll tell you, but before that, promise you won't judge me."

"Yes, I won't judge you. Just tell me her name."

"Okay then, her name is Namrah. I met her when we were in an expedition with Guruji."

"Wait!" I said. "You met her? She lives somewhere else?"

"Yes. Why?"

"How's that possible? Your species exists only in Gir National Park."

"That's not true. Our species lives far beyond the borders of this forest, but we have learned to keep low now."

"Okay. So what's the problem, is she aware of your feelings, and is she in love with you too?" I asked.

"Yes." He replied.

"You sure? Because it happens that girls often gives a signal of closeness to us and then throws us into the friend zone. Just be sure before you think ahead about this."

"Yes, yes. I am quite sure about it. We had a thing between us that only a close, very close relation, could have."

I do not know if an animal could blush or not, but if they could, this was definitely it. I gave him a naughty smile.

"Aha, that close ha?" I nudged him playfully.

"Stop it." He said. "This is extremely serious."

I got serious.

"So, what is problem between you both, you are both attracted to each other and you too already had a thing. So what is problem now? Are your parents not accepting this or what? "

"No, no, that's not the problem. We have not yet said anything to our parents about this."

"Then what's the problem." I asked.

He remained silent for a moment and then spoke again.

"The problem is that she is out of my league."

"What?!," I asked, "What do you mean by out of your league? You too already had a thing and now you realize that she is out of your league."

"You don't understand," he said, "it is not that simple. We kind of can't be together."

"Why, but?"

"She is not supposed to be with someone like me?"

"Why not?" I said. "You love her, she loves you. That's how this is supposed to be."

"No. It is not. It is not that simple."

"Why but, tell me the reason, tell me why you both can't be together?"

"Because," he said again ", she is not supposed to be with someone like me"

"Okay, Stop!" I said. "You are making this go round and round. Just tell me what the problem is and why you both can't be together."

"She is not what you think she is."

"You are losing me again." I said.

He thought for a moment and again spoke.

"What do you think she is?"

"A ferocious lioness with sharp claws and beautiful eyes and long shining tail that curls at the end and..."

"No, no," He stopped me in between, "...leave it. I will make it easy for you. She is not a lioness."

"What?" I said after the unexpected discovery. "She's not a lioness? Oh Man, don't tell me that SHE's a HE."

"No, no. She's a she but she's not a lioness."

"Okay than, what is she?"

"She's a tigress."

"Oh man, you must be kidding." I said.

"No. I am not kidding. She is a tigress. Intellectual, just like me, lives in Kanha, and is daughter of the chief of their tribe."

I was stunned. A lion was in love with a tigress. In animals, I thought, there could be nothing more complicated than this.

"You're crazy." I said.

"I know." He replied.

"Why do you have to love a tigress?" I asked. "You could love a lioness. Any lioness, form your tribe or another or anyone, but why tigress."

"I don't know." He replied. "I never wanted this, but still, it kind of just happened."

"How could it happen? You two are from two different species. Yours lives in pride and are social in nature. Whereas, hers, they live alone, they hunt alone, they eat alone, and they are not that social. Your pride lives for each other. If a lioness hunts down anything, they share it with whole pride. Whereas hers, they hunts for themselves and do not share their food with anyone. Tell me now, despite of all this differences, how could you fall in love with her?"

"I don't know. I never thought about it like that. It felt right to be with her and that is what I did. You yourself said that if I love her, and she loves me, that's how it is supposed to be."

"Yeah, I know, but I thought you were in love with some lioness. I had never thought it possible for a lion to be in love with a tigress."

"Aha. So what now? Knowing the things that I have told you, now it all changes, you change your words now?"

"No. I do not. I stick with my words. I just could not believe in your story. What do you want me to do?"

"I want you to give me an advice."

"For what?" I asked.

"Should I think about being with her? Would it be wrong if we loved each other? Is us being together, forbidden?"

"I don't know man. Humans still hesitate in marrying their children in different caste, and this is a case of completely different species. How am I supposed to advice you on this?"

"But still, you have been in love before and you are in love now, you can tell me what your heart says about it."

I remained silent. How am I supposed to say anything to him? He genuinely appears to be in love with the tigress. If I say anything to discourage him, it might break him down, and I do not want that. He had been a good friend to me and it was now my turn to return the favor.

"I don't know." I said. "This is all crazy. A lion and a tigress, in a love, that's a too much to believe for me even after this all that I had been through. However, personally, if you love her and she loves you, there is nothing for you to think about. Love is for soul, not for the bodies or castes. If you both are in love with each other, there is nothing wrong in that from my point of view. For others, I have no idea what they have to say about it. "

"Hmm. Thanks." He said. "Your opinion matters a lot to me. Thanks once again."

"Anytime," I replied. ", but before you take a step, you should talk to your father about this."

"Yeah. I will. Anyway, let us go to sleep now. It is too late and my father will be up early tomorrow for the march. "

"Yes. Let's get to sleep."

We stood there for a moment, and then, retired back to the cave.

Back in the cave, Kesari went to sleep in one of the corner. I too joined him and took him as support for my back. Soon my mind had escaped its boundaries and had drifted away into the infinite world of the beautiful dreams and unbelievable fantasies of lions and tigresses.

*

Next morning everyone was in rush. All had bid farewell to their families. As soon as sun had rose from the hills, twenty-six lions along with chief had started marching for the rescue operation. Only three lionesses had joined the operation, of which, one was Nrushikaji. Other than that, all remaining had stayed behind to take care of the elders and the kids.

I had asked Singh to join them to which he had clearly refused. I too, refused to go back to the caves. I wanted to be with them when they were in need. He asked me repeatedly to go back but I refused and hence, against my stubbornness, they agreed to take Kesari and me with them. I did this for Kesari. Everyone had it mind that Kesari was a coward, but I knew him better. So in order to clear up his reputation, I had undertaken this mission. He was glad that I did that. He wanted to join his father but could not directly disobey his father's command. This way, he will also follow his father's command and will be with him.

Pair of two lions walked few hundred meters in front to warn the group of any upcoming danger. Everyone including Singh took his or her turn of fifteen minutes in front. In this way, they got protection from any upcoming dangers and could walk in relaxation for long time.

No one spoke anything on the way. It was only Kesari and I, who were talking. We discussed different things and he told me few things that he had not said to me until now.

I checked for my knife while we were walking, but I could not find it anywhere. I asked Kesari if he had seen the knife to which he replied.

"It's there, right there, tucked in your trousers".

I searched for it but my hands could not find it. When I failed to locate the only weapon at my disposal for my safety, Kesari helped me and bought out the knife from my back. I took it in my hand and held it. Then again, I kept it back from where Kesari had bought it. The moment I kept it back, I again lost it and again, Kesari said that it was at the same place where it had been earlier.

By noon, we had reached the east part and Singh was in front. Everything was normal and there was no sign of danger. However, all of a sudden, we heard a roar from the front. We looked at the source and soon saw that left leg of the Singh was stuck in the toothed clamp.

All of us ran towards the Singh but before we could reach Singh, we heard sound of engines ascending from the forest. It appeared as if seven to eight Jeeps were on its way. Singh's roar might have given the poachers signal that they had captured a beast.

We were halfway there to the Singh when Singh shouted.

"Retreat." He said.

We all stopped and stood there not knowing what to do. From the other end of the forest, the noise of the engines got louder and louder.

"Retreat." Singh ordered again.

Everyone retreated except for Kesari and me. I turned to Kesari and saw tears rolling down from his eyes. I remembered how he had lost his mother, and right now, in same manner, today his father was asking him to leave. History was repeating itself.

"We must go. Kesari." I said.

"No. I can't lose my father now." He replied.

"Retreat." Singh ordered again.

"We must go. It's your father's command." I said.

He stood there looking at his father and after few moments, he finally turned. I climbed on his back and he galloped in the direction where all others had disappeared.

*

# CHAPTER 14

We met others in the trees. They were all lost in thoughts and there was a sense of tension in the air.

No one spoke anything. We sat there in-group. Everyone was in shock by the events that had taken place. Kesari was lost in thoughts. Nrushikaji sat next to us. She also was lost in thoughts. I was not sure of what to do. Therefore, I too sat there in silence.

"We must rescue him." Kesari said, breaking in the silence.

"But he had ordered us to retreat." One of the lion said.

"And we are nothing without him. We need a chief." Another one added.

All of them debated of what to do. However, in the end, all of them fell silent again not knowing what to do.

"We should call Makata." One of them said.

All agreed as it appeared logical. It was what other lions did to rescue the one who was caught.

"He wouldn't appear." Kesari Said. "Or else we wouldn't have been here. It is because of his absence that we are here. Any one of the seven would have tried that, and he must have called us earlier if he had sensed any great danger. We cannot rely on him."

"Then what should we do?" asked Nrushikaji.

"I don't know." Replied Kesari. "Only thing I know is that my father is caught and we need to rescue other seven lions along with him and Nrushikaji's husband."

We stood there in silence. We had nothing to do. No one had any plan, and above this all, we had no leader to follow.

"Someone must enter their camp." I said.

I had their attention now. All had their ears fixed on me.

"I have an idea." I continued, ", when it starts getting dark, you all chase me to their camp. I will run directly into their camp as someone who is running away from lions. Once in their camp, I will tell them that I had seen group of large number of lions and they had chased me everywhere. Being poachers, they will ask me to show them where lions were. However, at that time, it already will be dark and I will tell them that I will show the lion's location in the morning. They will have no other option but to accept it. At night, I will free the captured ones, and run away with them from the camp. In this way we can free all of them and no one will get hurt in the process."

"We can't risk your life." Kesari said.

"Do we have any other choice?" I asked.

No one said anything.

"How will we find the camp?" asked Kesari.

"Leave it to me." Nrushikaji said. "I will find it."

No one objected to her. She was the eldest among us and was wife of the bravest amongst them, and everyone knew that she would do anything for her husband. Hence, everyone agreed to it.

"Then it's settled." Said Kesari. "Until it gets dark, Nrushikaji will search the camp and we will call out for Makata. If he appears, then there will be no need for Shiv to enter the camp. If he doesn't, we will stick to Shiv's plan."

All of them agreed. We were twenty-four in number excluding Nrushikaji. We split up into six groups. Kesari looked up in the sky, at sun.

"It is three right now. We all will meet here at around six. Be cautious and lookout for traps. I don't want anyone trapped. Now let's proceed."

Every group disappeared in different direction. I, Kesari, Sambha and one other lion remained on our position along with Nrushikaji.

"Take care." I said to Nrushikaji. "I don't want to lose my mother, again."

She smiled at me. Then she turned and disappeared in the direction from which we had ran. Once she was gone, we too started moving.

During all the time that we had, we searched for Makata. We scanned trees, looked in grass, called out for him, but he was nowhere. I had no idea of how Makata looked nor did Kesari, but Sambha knew Makata and every time we pointed at a monkey, he just said no. He said that Makata could be easily distinguished from these wild monkeys. He said we would recognize him, once we had all seen him. Therefore, in the end we stopped pointing at monkeys because all appeared same to us. In the end, we failed in locating the Makata. We had called out for him, but there was no response from his side. At the end, we had no other option but to move back to the meeting place.

As minutes ticked by, other groups returned. Time passed by and every group was back. No one had any lead on Makata's whereabouts. We sat there and waited for Nrushikaji. She was the only one who had not returned. We sat there in silence. Time continued to pass by but Nrushikaji did not return. It was getting dark now and still Nrushikaji had not returned.

I thought that, we might have made mistake by sending her. She might be in some danger or had been captured by the Poachers. I felt worried and thought of asking Kesari to call out for her, but then, I spotted her in the distance. I sighed in relief on seeing her.

She walked to us and sat next to Kesari. She was panting and taking deep breaths. Everyone was waiting for her to say something.

"I found them." She said finally.

"They are around five kilometers from here. The camp is heavily guarded and is much tougher to get in. The numbers of poachers are high. Around fifty to sixty and above it, they got large ammunition with them. Walking into it is like walking into the death. They have kept too many traps all around the camp except for the front gate from where vehicles enter the camp."

"What to do then?" asked Kesari.

"We will stick to the plan." I said.

"How do we know where trap is laid?" I asked to Nrushikaji.

"You will see a bit of iron peeking out from the land. That is the center for the clamp." she said.

"Fine then. I want you all to stop chasing me as soon as Nrushikaji gives the clue that traps had started. That way, you all can be out from the range of bullets, and any other harm. Once I am in the camp, I want you to move back so that you all are safe."

Every one sat there listening to the plan that I was narrating. Once I had narrated the plan, we sat there waiting for sun to go down.

After some time, I stood from my place and looked up at the sky. It was early but soon it will start getting dark.

"It's time now. Let's start it."

I started walking and everyone followed me.

"Stop." I said. "I want you to chase me as if I am a prey. I don't want you all to follow me."

I started again.

Everyone stood there on his or her place.

Distance between us grow with every step. In the end, they were only dots in the distance. Then they started running. I too started the sprint. I tried to run as fast as possible but at same time kept eye on ground for any traps.

Soon I was running through the trees.

Behind me, I heard roar of angry lions.

They were playing their part well.

I kept on running.

Perspiration ran down my face and still there was no sign of any camp.

Then finally, through the branches, I saw a glimpse of the camp.

I kept on running.

I turned and saw the lions few meters behind me. They had covered the distance rapidly.

Soon I was in front of the camp. I stopped and covered myself behind trees. The guards were on alert. They must have heard the roars. I searched for the main gate and when I located it, I ran directly towards it. I turned and saw the lions still following me. However, all of a sudden they all came to a halt. On the gate, two men appeared with guns in their hands.

They fired the shots at beasts, but lions were far from the range of the bullets. On hearing the gunshots, they turned back and disappeared into the forest. Once they were gone, both gunman turned to me. They caught me from sleeve and dragged me into the camp to one of the cabin.

They threw me into the cabin. One of the gunman followed me whereas other one stood outside. In front of me was a table and behind the table was a chair. Someone sat there reading the newspaper spreading out his legs on the table.

"Captain!" said the gunman.

The occupant of the chair peeped out from the paper. Then he kept the paper aside and stood up from the chair. He was a well-muscled man. He picked up the cigar from the table and moved placed it between his lips.

"Captain, this boy ran into the camp while he was chased by a pride of lions."

"Is that so?" he asked me.

"Yeah. I had no other option." I said.

"Why were they following you?" He asked me.

"I don't know why, but as soon as the group of lion saw me, they started running after me. I was too far for them to catch me immediately, so I ran. After that, I saw the camp from the trees. Therefore, I came here before they can put their claws on me. As soon as they were near the camp area, these guys fired at them and as a result the group retreated and I was saved."

"How did you end up in the forest?" asked the captain with suspicion.

"One evil man with a gun threw me from a waterfall." I replied. "Since then I am searching for a way out and had accidently bumped into this group of lions. Since then, they were after me and I was running away from them. I wanted to get out of this forest and was hoping that you could show me a way out of this mess."

"We will help you, if you help us." He said. "Do you remember where you saw the lions?"

Yes. This was it. Everything was working out as I had predicted.

"Yeah. But I can't figure out the spot in dark." I said.

"Then we will look out in the morning. After that we will take you out of this jungle."

"Thank you." I said.

"Actually, I should thank you." He said.

"Give him a tent to rest at night." He said to the gunman.

"And one more thing," I said. "Can I get something to eat?"

He smiled and nodded at the gunman. We left the tent and moved to the right. Many of the tents here were big enough to hold big cages. I heard few low pained growls from the right most tent. Two man stood there with guns.

That must be the main cage tent.

We stopped in front of a tent that was fourth to the cage tent.

We entered the tent.

The only things in the tent were sleeping bags and few backpacks.

"No one will be here tonight so it's all yours." Gunman said. "Make yourself comfortable while I arrange something for you to eat."

The gunman left the room. I sat there and made myself comfortable.

After few minutes, the gunman reappeared with a plate of fruits. He handed me the plate and again left.

I ate the fruits that was not as delicious as the fruits at the caves, but it satiated my hunger. Once I felt filled, I drank water from bottle that was given to me along with the fruits.

I scanned the room. I sat there and relaxed myself. Thoughts filled my mind and I let them flow. I thought of everything that had happened until now. Falling from the waterfall, coming face to face with crocodiles, meeting Kesari, encounter with Guruka, our journey to the council, meeting with Nrushikaji.

Everything that was happening was so hard to believe, yet it was all true. I thought of my friends and Shivani how she would have reacted if she had been on my place. I thought of the way she had sung songs at college carnivals. I wondered how it would have turned out if I had not fell for her. It would have been dull and colorless life.

I closed my eyes and thought of the day when I had first told Vaishavi about my feelings. I wished that day had never come in my life and as I closed my eyes, the glimpses of that day filled my mind. I forced them away and thought of other things to keep my mind busy. I focused on the task in my hand and thought of the ways to execute my plan. I kept on thinking and thinking until I had lost track of time and soon I was fast asleep despite of all the things that were going around me.

*

# CHAPTER 15

When I opened my eyes again, it was very dark. I looked at the watch that was on the table. It was 1:00 AM.

I got up and peeped out. Everything was silent. Only few tents had its lights on. Few guards were on guard. Other than that, there was complete silence. This was my chance.

I slipped out of the tent from the rear. I felt cold steel tucked in my trousers. It was the knife. It had somehow, again reappeared at my rescue. I walked in the shadows keeping myself out of view. One after another, I passed every tent, and soon I was at the last tent.

I slowly entered the tent with knife in my hand. It was completely dark inside. I held my position until my eyes got used to the dark, everything got clear. There were few cages. Some of them were empty, some of them had lions and one that was closest to me had a monkey.

"Shiv?!" said one of the lion.

"Singh." I said recognizing the voice.

"I am here to free you."

I went to the closest cage.

"Are you Makata?" I asked the monkey.

"Yes, that's me." He said.

I started working on unbolting the cage locks. Slowly and steadily, the bolts came out and soon I had opened the first cage, and the monkey got free. Then next cage. Then again next cage. One by one, I had opened eight cages and freed seven lions and a monkey. Then I opened the Singh's cage. Soon all of them were out except for Guruka.

"Promise me you won't attack me this time." I tried to make a joke with Guruka. However, he did not laugh.

I started opening the bolt.

"Hey what are you doing?" said the guard, who had entered the tent, while I was unbolting the cage. He was about to fire a shot at me, when I jumped at him.

"You all get out." I said to Singh and others but they did not move.

"Help!" screamed the guard.

"Go now! Or you won't get another chance." I said.

This time, all of them ran. I heard gunshots outside.

While I was battling, or to be precise, struggling with the guard on the ground, another guard came in. Seeing me in fight with the guard, he hit me on the head with back of his gun. As a result, I lost the conscious and everything got dark around me.

212

*

When I opened my eyes, I was in the cagewhich had earlier captivated Singh. It was early in the morning. In cage next to me was Guruka.

I sat there in the cage holding my head in my hands. The pain was tremendous for me to bear.

"So are you going to apologize to me?" I asked Guruka.

"Why should I?" Guruka asked in response.

"For attacking me." I said.

"No. I'm never going to apologize to a human." He said.

"You will. Anyway, Nrushikaji already apologized me and I already forgave you."

"You met my wife?" he asked.

"Yeah and she is my mother now."

"What? Your mother?"

"Yeah. She accepted me as her son. Now only thing I need is father."

"I'm not going to be your father." He said immediately.

"I didn't ask. And I don't want a father who is always thirsty for my blood." I said laughing at my own comment.

I wanted this conversation to be as light as possible.

He remained silent.

I too sat in silence after that.

Few moments passed without a word, and then again, I spoke.

"I'm sorry for your son."

He remained silent.

"I don't know if I should say this or not but you know what, you should stop acting like this."

"I don't need to learn to act from you. It is your kind because of whom I am acting like this today."

"Yeah I know it's because of our kind but we all are not the same."

"It doesn't matter."

"No, it does. Maybe it does not matter to you, all others, or me, but it does to your family. Do you know how much your wife is suffering because of you?"

"No. She is not suffering because of me. She is suffering because of your kind. Your kind took her son away from her. Do you know how it feels to lose your son? To lose someone you love?"

I remained silent. Deep within me, I felt the emptiness again that I hadalways wished to fill. Face of Vaishavi, face of my parents, appeared in front of me eyes.

"I don't know how it feels to lose a son you love, but I do know how it feels to lose someone you love, someone you trust, and someone who takes your care." I said.

I closed my eyes and again those three faces appeared in front of me whom I had missed the most.

"I lost my parents when I was still a kid." I said.

"They had come to drop me at hostel," I continued, ", and on that day, while returning, they met with an accident."

Tears rolled down from my eyes. I wiped those tears out, but again, another pair of tears took their place.

"That wasn't your fault." Guruka said.

"You don't know it all." I said.

"This thing I had never told to anyone, not even to my best friends. Only Vimal knows partially about it. I never talk about this with anyone but I feel I should tell this to you. You are doing what I had once done.

From first day of my school, I loved a girl named Vaishavi. We were in same class. I used to watch her laugh, smile, talk, and enjoy. I enjoyed those days of school. I always waited for school to reopen so that I could see her again. Those were best days of my childhood. I used to visualize her in ponytails, with lose hairs, with buns. I used to steal a glimpse of her whenever I had a chance. I always wondered how wonderful it would have been if we had held each other's hands when we had come to school. I was always so lost in her and that made me feel good.

However that all was soon over. I had passed my seventh grade and from the eighth grade, I was to live in the boarding school. I told her about my feelings and asked her for her love in return. She refused my proposal because she was already been told to someone else. I was broken, depressed, and sent to another school. When I came back home again, I went to her home to find it locked. I learned that her family had moved to London. It led me to more depression. When I was sent back to hostel, I missed her and it depressed me. Out of depression, I tried to kill myself by slipping my leg from the stairs.

Due to that accident, I was sent back home. Back at the home, I used to lock myself in my room and cry for hours in her memories. My parents had no idea of what was going on with me. They were worried. They always asked me for the reason behind this kind of behavior to which I remained silent. Soon I had recovered from the injuries and was sent back to hostel. On that day, my parents had come to drop me at the hostel and it was then, that, while returning, they died in an accident."

I sat there as I gave in to the tears. I was sobbing heavily.

"If I wouldn't have acted like that, my parents would have been alive now. My parents had died because of me. I was the reason of their death. I had ignored their love for me and had cried for the love that I never had in my life."

I cried and cried and cried to let my pain out. When I was too tired to cry anymore, I sat there in silence. After few seconds of total silence between Guruka and me, Guruka finally spoke.

"I'm sorry for your parents." Guruka said.

"No. You don't understand." I said. "It isn't about me. It's about you. You are doing what I had once done. In my love for Vaishavi, I had ignored all the love that I had received from my parents, and now when they are gone, I am longing for their love, which I am never going to get back. In search for the love that I never had, I lost the one that I already had, and right now, you are doing the same thing.

Your love for your son is keeping you away from the love you have. I am not saying you should forget your son. You should remember him but in memories that brings you joy.

I have seen love for you in your wife's eyes, and emptiness she holds in your absence. She really loves you a lot but you are ignoring her and not loving her back. She is so strong that she is still waiting for you but I request you to not test her strength anymore. Every strength has a limit, and every wait has a time. If you lose her once, you will never have her back. You just need to love her back. She doesn't need anything else from you."

To all the things that I had told him, he remained silent.

"I promised her that I will bring her husband that she craved for, back to her." I said. "But I don't know if I can. It is up to you. Whether you want to make your family happy or not."

After that, I said nothing and we both sat in silence. Few moments later, a guard came in the tent.

Seeing me back in the conscious, he left the tent again and reappeared with the captain.

"So you were their rescuer." Said the captain.

He gestured the guard to leave and the guard obeyed.

"I don't need them anymore. We are not here for them. We are here for something far more valuable that their skin. Something that is going to change my life forever. We are here to learn few secrets that this forest beholds, and now, when you are with these dumb animals, it appears that you already know few. So the question now is will you share it the soft way or the hard way."

"I don't know what you are talking about?" I said.

"Then why did you help the lions escape?" he asked.

"Oh that. I thought poaching is illegal and so I just did it to stop the poaching. Kind of social service, you know."

"You speak a lot," he said, ", but not what I want. You don't understand what I will do to you."

"You think I know few things? Then I say I do. Not few but a lot. But you are not going to learn anything from me."

"You are stupid. You will regret for this and pay for your decision Shiv Patel." He said.

"Wait, how do you know my name?" I asked him.

"I know much more," he said, "I know more about you than you think. You have same stubbornness as your stupid parents. They were the most foolish couple I had ever come across."

"You don't know my parents. They were the best people that I have ever known."

"Oh, is that so? Then where are they right now." He said.

"They died in an accident years ago."

"They did? You sure?" he asked.

"Yes. I am. This is my parents you are talking about; there is no reason for me for not being sure. I mourned their death and cremated their bodies with my own hands. I cried day and night for their loss. I have missed them every moment of my life until date and still I hope to see them. Yet, I know that they are not coming back because I know what is once gone is gone forever. Dead never rise again."

"Hmm, then I must have been mistaken all this year. I see them every year and still you say they are dead. May be you are right or maybe I am, but whatever it is, this is not good for them in any way."

"What are you saying? You are bluffing. This cannot be true. If my parents had been alive, they would never stay away from me. I know them. They cannot stay away from their son, their only son."

"If that's the case, you don't know your parents at all. If what you say is true and if what I say is lie, then this photo should also be some lie."

He showed me a photograph in his cell phone in which a man and woman, who looked like my parents, were trying to blend in the crowd of some business dressed people, in a foreign location.

"That's computer graphics." I said. "This cannot be true. You are making this all up to get to me."

"Believe what you want to. In any case, your days are numbered; you are going to die along with you parents. Mr. Gem never lets anyone live who crosses his path, and you are standing between him and his biggest dream that...."

Gunshots interrupted him. He left the tent to learn what was wrong out there.

As soon as he was out, Makata, the monkey, entered from the rear.

"Hi, what's up?" He spoke.

"Not having the fun! Now stop questioning and get to work. The cage is locked and I need to get out."

"Not to worry!" He said and bought out a bunch of keys from somewhere.

"Ha-Ha! You are just incredible. Now open the lock. Fast."

He opened the lock and soon I was free. I heard few more gunshots.

"You set Guruka free, while I see what's happening."

"Don't worry, my team have control over the situation and Singh and his team is on the way." Makata said.

Ignoring him, I stepped out. The scene that lay out in front of me was not under control in any sense. There were hundreds of monkeys all over the camp. Every guard was struggling with one, two, or few of them. Some were trying to shoot at them but they were jumping all over the place. It was difficult for guards to aim. I saw captain running past the struggling guards.

I laughed seeing the guards struggling with the monkeys. Captain had somehow made its way through all struggling guards. He disappeared into his tent and again reappeared holding the firecrackers. He lighted a fire-rocket and the rocket busted out in the sky with a deafening noise. As a result, all the monkeys started running away in the shock. Within moments all the monkeys were gone leaving my laughter and me alone with fear. I closed my eyes and remembered the way, how, Ranchoddas Shyamaldas Chanchad a.k.a Rancho, had fooled his heart in 3-idiots movie.

"Aal iss Well…Aal iss Well…" I said to my heart.

Captain's eyes turned to me and he called out his guard to capture me.

The guard, who was nearest to me, ran, and tried to get his grip around me. However, even before he could put his hands on me, a shadowy figured appeared over my head and flattened the guard on the ground.

It was Guruka. He had jumped over my height, directly on the guard with his jaw at his neck. The guard was dead even before he had realized what has happened. Then, Guruka stood next to me.

"He isn't alone." He said.

At that point, what the guards heard was only a low angry growl.

Every gun in the camp had turned to Guruka and me. As if we both were not enough, Makata jumped out of the tent directly on my soldier.

"That bloody monkey." Shouted the captain. "Shoot all of them."

I heard a shot but none of us fell onto the ground. Instead one of the guard on right fell. I turned to the direction from which the shot came, and saw a helicopter flying towards us. At the doors was a man with a rowdy moustache holding a sniper.

"Shoot at helicopter." shouted the captain.

Getting the command, every gun started firing at the helicopter, but it was too far to aim. Seeing so many bullets fired at them, the chopper kept on changing positions. Guards kept on firing. Seeing guards distracted, Guruka and I ran for the front gate. Guruka was faster than I was so he was soon out of the camp through front gate. It was my turn now.

"Stop him." Called out captain seeing me running away.

One of the guard blocked my path. He pointed his gun at me, but before he could shoot, a lion grabbed him from his neck and after two swirls threw him on other guard. Then it turned to me.

"Need any help?" Kesari asked.

"Yeah, I was waiting for your team only."

Soon all others along with Guruka entered the battlefield. Now the guards were facing ferocious lions along with bullets from the sky.

Seeing the guards dying, Captain disappeared in his tent and reappeared holding a gun. He targeted the lion, the most fearsome and majestic lion of all, with his gun and fired a shot.

The bullet hit the target and Guruka scrambled to the ground. Seeing his target down, captain pointed on a lioness.

Meanwhile seeing Guruka on ground, I searched for the source. At same time, Kesari had already found the source and was running at him. Soon I too found captain holding the gun with his next target on Nrushikaji.

I ran at Nrushikaji while Kesari ran for captain.

Captain, who had locked his target, fired the shot and I, at same time, dived at Nrushikaji.

Once I was up again, I looked at Nrushikaji.

She was all right.

I was glad nothing had happened to her, but then, all of a sudden, I felt the pain in my stomach. I moved my hand to my stomach and found it wet with hot blood, that was bursting out from the hole that bullet had made.

Seeing my blood, I started losing the sight. I turned to the direction from where the bullet was shot, but everything was dark in front of me.

Then my sight returned and I saw Guruka on top of the captain and his jaws on captain's neck.

I again lost my sight, and when it returned, I saw a chopper landing on the ground.

Again, I lost my sight and when it came back, I was three feet above the ground.

I saw all the lions and lioness standing there with their eyes filled with tears.

Then, my sight was blurred and it was completely dark all around me. I tried to open my eyes again, but it remained dark. I tried to get a glimpse of the light but darkness prevailed. Soon, I felt my heartbeats slowing down too and my thoughts, which were racing in all direction, were finally slowing its pace down and getting still. With every passing moment, I got more and more close to making peace with my life and facing the death. I was closing down to death and there were still so many answers that I still had to find. I prayed to god to keep me alive and survive this situation. I prayed, prayed, and prayed until there came the final moments when there was only one thing I could do any further.

Let the time do its job and death do it's. There was nothing now that I could do.

*

# CHAPTER 16

When I opened my eyes, an ivory colored fan was revolving in a center of a white ceiling. It took time for my eyes to adjust to new environment.

The first thing that came to my mind was lions. It appeared, as if, all that had happened was in a dream. May be nothing had happened at all. I must be sleeping in the room at Leo resort.

Then I heard beeping sound. All of a sudden pain erupted from nowhere in my stomach. As my eyesight got clear, I saw a bottle hanging upside down on a pipe from which a liquid was passing all the way to my hand and into my body through syringe. I tried to get up but as soon as I tried, pain shot through my spine.

"Stay still." Said a male voice.

I turned to the source and saw a man with heavy muscles and rowdy moustache, seating next to me with his head in a book. His face seemed to be familiar. Then everything got clear to me.

I was in hospital and the man was one who had come to our rescue in a chopper. I remembered the camp. The captain, the guards, the cages, freeing the lions, then getting caught, Makata freeing us, the monkeys, arrival of chopper, running away, the lions, Kesari killing the guard, captain firing, Guruka getting shot… and then it was all blur.

"What happened to Guruka?" I asked the man.

"Sorry?!" he asked astonished

"I mean what happened to the lion that was shot?"

"Oh him. He is all right. He is back to the forest but under supervision. It was amazing how rapidly he is recovering from the injuries."

"Yeah, they are amazing." I said.

I thought of the facts that I knew that others did not. If they ever came to know of the facts, they would not believe any of them.

"So what do you know that we don't?" he asked.

"Nothing." I said immediately.

"C'mon. Don't fool me." He said and kept his book down,

"I know they are different from all other animals, but I don't know how. I want to know why they exist. I want to help them but I do not know how. I have no idea of what they are, why they are or what they do, or whatever they do. The only thing I know is that I owe them a debt."

"You owe them debt? How?" I asked.

"Yes. I owe them a life." He replied.

"I'm not getting what you are saying."

"My name is Vikram Rathore and I'm a forest officer. Few years back, I was posted in the Gir national park. I worked in the park for a year and then received my transfer letter to Kanha National Park.

It was while leaving the forest that I was standing at the station of Sasan Gir with my wife. My kid was playing next to us. My wife and I got busy in talking and forgot about our child's location. Then, I heard honking from the train engine and started searching for my son. At time when we had realized that he was on the track, it was too late. We thought that we were going to lose him, but all of sudden a lion emerged from nowhere and caught my son just before he was about to get hit.

That day I realized that someone superior than us, exist, and to know what it was, I got my posting back to Gir. Again, I saw the same lion with you at the camp and it confirms that you know more than you are pretending. If they weren't any different, then you wouldn't have survived alone in the forest."

"Sometimes it is good if you don't know few things." I said. "Knowing things, hurts."

"I don't get what you say." He said confused.

I thought for a moment to decide, if I should say anything to him or not. Once I had made up my mind, I continued.

"The lion you saw next to me in the camp was the same lion that had saved your son. The day he saved your son, his son was killed by a train."

He remained silent to what I had said. He had no idea of what I was saying and confusion was very visible on his face.

"The day he saves a life of a kid of a human, human takes away life of his kid. You think if I tell you the secret that I behold; you will be able to help them. No. It will not help them. The more the people know about them, the more the danger they face. More hunters and poachers will come in for them. The one we killed at the camp knew that they held some secrets and that is why they were capturing them. So if you really want to help them, help them all. Not only those lions, but all."

He remained silent. He then took out a recorder from his pocket and kept it on bed.

"I need to take your report on how you ended up in the forest." He said. "The guide, the guard and the driver says that you were taking photos at the dam when they were in the checkpoint. When they came out, you were gone and nowhere to be seen. Your friends say the same thing but I feel something missing. I need to listen to the truth from you."

"The truth? The truth is that I was thrown away from that checkpoint by that man with the gun."

"Which man?" he asked surprised.

"The man with gun, the one who sat in front with the guide and the guard in the Geep."

"There was no one there in the front except for the driver in the driver's seat and guide and guard in the conductor's."

"No. There was." I objected. "There was a man with a gun who sat next to the guide. He was there the whole time."

"No. There was not. If there was, then your friends too would be lying along with the guide, the guard and the driver."

"Wait! My friends too said it was only them, driver, guard and the guide. They mentioned no one with a gun."

"No. Why?"

"Oh man, how is that possible? There was this man with a gun. He fought with me, threw me off from that dam, and tried to shoot me at the waterfall when I was trying to get back. Wait, I had his knife with me if you need it for a proof."

"What knife?" he asked again.

"The knife, you didn't find the knife at the camp. It should have been next to me. I had it."

"Sorry, but we found no knife with you at the camp. You were there all bare hand. You had no weapon at your disposal, and maybe, if you had it, it could have been anywhere at the camp in that situation. Whatever it is, right now, you rest. I will send an artist later to you to get a sketch of that man of whom you speak. Once we have the sketch ready, we can easily get to the men whoever is behind this all."

He turned the recorder off and kept it back in his pocket.

"Apart from that," he continued, "I need to inform you that you cannot go to any of the forest in the country until further notice is issued to you by the forest department. Once it is proved that you had no hand in any kind of poaching activities or any relation with poachers, restriction laid on you will be revoked, and you will be free to enter the forests." he said.

"The poachers you had faced were working for someone whom they were calling Mr. Gem. Do you know anything about him?"

The word Gem bought everything in front of my eyes. The reason of the existence of the lions, the story that was told to me, everything, but I was supposed to keep that to myself.

"Nope. Nothing." I said.

"Ok, but you need to be careful. Your life is still in danger. Whoever this Mr. Gem is, he is surely going to come back to you."

"I'll take care." I said.

"Okay. I will send someone for your protection in minutes. You better take rest for now."

He stood up and moved to the door. He opened the door to leave.

"And one more thing. You can contact me whenever you need any kind of help."

"Thanks for the offer. I'll keep it in mind." I said with a smile.

He left the room closing the door behind him. I relaxed on my bed. The softness of the bed felt good. I closed my eyes and thought about past few days in the jungle. I thought about Kesari, Singh, Nrushikaji and the image of Makata bought smile on my face. Then I remembered what the captain of the camp had said about my parents being alive. I wondered if the photo that he had showed me was a real photo or some computer graphics. If it was original, I wondered where my parents were. I wanted to know what they were up to, and why they were staying away from the only son they had. I wanted to ask them why they had left me in all the misery and pain that I had to go through because of their death.

"You feeling good" said a female voice, interrupting all of my thoughts.

I opened my eyes and saw a nurse working on the monitors.

"Yeah," I said. "Just thinking about some stuff."

"Good stuff or bad stuff?" she asked.

"Don't know. Maybe good and bad both."

"Hmm. That is something like I have heard about you. Anyway I have a message for you."

"What message?" I asked not knowing what this nurse was talking about.

For a moment, the nurse stood in front of me without saying anything. She took out her spectacles, and cleansed the lens with a handkerchief from her pocket. Once she had cleansed her spectacles, she wore them back and gave a smile that in all manner appeared cruel and evil to me. After that she said,

"Mr. Gem says Hi!"

\*

After few minutes, another nurse ran to the doctor. She had no idea of how this all had happened but whatever it was, doctor required to check it immediately.

"What is it?" Doctor asked.

"The patient from the forest, he needs your immediate attention." she said.

The doctor hurried to the patient from the forest's room.

Outside the room, Aastha, Smit, Visha, Dimpu, Vimal, Brijesh, Jigar and everyone else of them were waiting for the news from the doctor. However, the sudden rush from the doctor had made them to worry for their friend. They had no idea of why Shiv was shot and what his actual condition was. All they knew was that, their friend was facing a life-death situation.

Moments passed by and doctor came out of the room.

Aastha rushed to the doctor and asked.

"How's he? Is he awake?"

Doctor took a look at all of Shiv's friend. Their face awaiting answer. He had, an hour ago, left the room with a hope that the Shiv's condition will improve. However, god knows how, something had gone wrong and everything that they had tried in order to save the patient's life was in vain. The doctor turned to the girl in front of him, who was asking for her friend. He wanted to tell him that he was fine but he had to tell them the truth.

Doctor took the deep breath and looked into the girl's eyes.

"I'm sorry." He said. "The friend you have known, is no more."

*

To be continued...

## ABOUT THE AUTHOR

Sanket is a big fan of cartoon and animation. He is often found watching Pixar and Disney Movies in his free time. With a keen interest for paintings and softwares, he is a kind of a creative geek that wants to make something out of his mind. He is an ordinary person with extra-ordinary visions to make anything possible and hence, is always lost in his own world of ideas that can change lives.

Sanket lives in Nadiad, and has completed his graduation from CHARUSAT. He currently works as a freelancer, and develops and designs mobile, computer, and web applications for indiviuals and firms.